MY
GIFT
TO YOU

MY
GIFT
TO YOU

A Novel

Lori Nawyn

Covenant Communications, Inc.

This book is dedicated with love and respect to my
Grandma Minnie, who taught me about kindness. And to
my great-grandmother Maggie Ipsen, of Corinne, Utah, who
sent me to meet the woman in the basement house.

Cover image *Gift Box* © Kutaytanir, courtesy iStockphoto.

Cover design copyrighted 2010 by Covenant Communications, Inc.

Published by Covenant Communications, Inc.
American Fork, Utah

ted in Canada
Printing: October 2010

4 13 12 11 10   10 9 8 7 6 5 4 3 2 1

978-1-60861-101-0

ACKNOWLEDGMENTS

With heartfelt gratitude, I acknowledge the patience of family and friends who have supported me in my desire to write. Thanks to Bethany for blessing me with knowledge, Sara for believing in me long before it was merited, and my Aunt Bass for cheering me on. Thanks also to Sherralynn Arnold for remedying my attempts at Spanish, and to Brandon Freeman, Cinzia Noble, and Meg Ferry for their help with the Spanish and Latin pronunciations for the audio version of the book. Special thanks to Tristi Pinkston for her sharp eyes and friendship—without her, I'd still have a heart full of words and not know what I could do with them.

PROLOGUE

December 20, 2009

TRISH INGRAM PRESSED HER LIPS together into a rigid line as she paced the tiled entryway of her two-story home. Gone was her hard-edged confidence. In its place stirred a whirlwind of emotional distress. She hated losing control, and no one threatened her composure more than her sister-in-law, Jamie. It was more than their discordant personalities. More than the way Jamie dressed, making her look like a woman with whom Trish wouldn't usually associate.

There was something else.

Trish stopped pacing and stood with her hands on her hips. Why did even the very thought of Jamie make her feel so unraveled? She struggled to draw a breath of air. Besides the fact that Jamie reminded her of a multitude of things she wanted to forget, part of her apprehension stemmed from a simple reality: Jamie was dying.

Striding toward the expansive living room that opened to the left of the entry, Trish nervously patted her hair. Sprayed into submission, the shoulder length strands—the color of which her stylist called "honey-kissed auburn"—barely moved at her touch. She attempted to force a look of confidence onto her perfectly made-up face, but fear eroded her resolve.

She paused inside the archway that separated the entry from the living room. On the far wall of the entryway hung an enormous mirror. She'd had it placed there so people entering the room could check their clothing and makeup if they desired.

Each time she studied herself in this or any mirror, Trish stared hard, searching for the attributes she'd worked to cultivate. Did she reflect the life she'd painstakingly pieced together from studying the lives of the other women she deemed strong and successful? Women whose photos she had collected in her teenage years, as well as in times of angst and self-doubt since, and taped to the mirror of the old dresser in the attic. She did it as if doing such a thing could really help mold her into the kind of person she'd convinced herself she needed to become.

She covered her face with her hands and shook her head, dismissing the childish perception. Even thoughts of the idiosyncrasies she utilized to survive must be kept under lock and key in the depths of her soul. No one would ever understand the true elements that made up her life, especially someone like Jamie.

Trish let her hands fall to her sides as she walked into the living room and peered out the front windows. The persistent drizzle of a late December storm pelted the morning, the gray sky gloomy and dark like her mood. Why had Jamie phoned and insisted on paying her a visit? No one had heard from her in almost two weeks.

Jamie's timing couldn't be worse.

In five days, it would be Christmas. The holiday season was a time to forget worries and be happy—no—blissful. Having everything planned, prepared, and running like clockwork was Trish's idea of bliss. She spun around on the heel of her pumps and surveyed her surroundings, folding her arms across her chest. She smiled in satisfaction. Just like the homes featured in top décor magazines, her house and everything in it was enviably posh.

Visible through a wide hallway and set of triple arches on the west of the living room, extravagantly wrapped gifts were arranged under a hand-decorated Christmas tree that towered the full two-story height of the family room. A matching set of three trees in the living room boasted expensive ornaments from Switzerland. Wreaths and garlands decorated every other room in the house. The fragrances of pine and spice drifting from glowing candles added an airborne elegance.

Trish sat down on the edge of the sofa. Yes, she sighed, a few more presents and another couple of dozen cookies for the neighbors—who always raved over her mouth-watering gingerbread—and she'd be finished. She'd pull off the perfect

Christmas. Anticipated holiday bliss was only several hundred dollars and three batches of cookies away—at least up until a few minutes ago.

Until the phone call from Jamie.

Jamie . . .

Like a parent trying to protect a child from danger, Trish tried to steer her mind from a path bordered on each side by daggers of fright. There were things about Jamie she allowed herself to be cognizant of, things she could only half-acknowledge, and things that were just too overpowering to fully absorb. Jamie had leukemia—that fact could not be avoided or ignored—a type that was particularly virulent and which would shortly take her life.

Yet, for some reason, Jamie had chosen to abandon her husband, Mike, and her stepdaughter, Stephanie, and had taken to the road in her car, probably traveling about like some errant hippie. As far as Trish knew, Jamie hadn't bothered to let anyone know her whereabouts or even if she was still alive. Far worse for Trish, Jamie had plied her with questions before her departure. Questions she'd avoided answering. Questions Jamie had no business asking.

Does Jamie know?

She tensed, then forced her thoughts in another direction. The fact was that Jamie's leaving so suddenly and without word was self-centered and thoughtless. The disregard she obviously had for Mike and Stephanie filled Trish with indignation.

How could a mother so selfishly discard those she was supposed to love?

Trish's tightly reigned emotions clamored like demons waiting to be unleashed. Tears burned the back of her eyes, but she refused to let them escape. Didn't Jamie realize how her careless choices had damaged the lives of her family?

All too soon, Trish heard the metallic screech of Jamie's rusted green Chevy. She rose to her feet and steeled herself, fervently hoping her neighbors were still asleep or, at least, otherwise occupied. Whatever it was Jamie wanted, Trish had to get this over with—fast.

Wearing a pair of dangling snowman earrings, Jamie emerged from her car and stumbled forward on a pair of black platform heels. Her faded denim jacket opened to a tight shirt emblazoned with a surfboarding Santa.

Trish watched through the rain-spattered windows in the living room, then moved stiffly into the entry. She jerked open the front door before Jamie had a chance to ring the bell.

"Jamie. How good to see you," she blurted, trying not to grimace.

"I won't come in," Jamie announced, running her hand through the thinning tendrils of her short red hair.

Trish stood firm and nodded, hoping Jamie wouldn't change her mind.

"Trish, do you remember when Mike and I got married?" Jamie didn't wait for a reply. "There we were, in the courthouse—me not looking like much of a bride—and in you came with this ridiculously huge bouquet of white roses. Mike had told me about my stuffy sister-in-law-to-be who never thought anyone or anything was good enough. I thought, *Great. She thinks she'll spruce me up a little by shoving a white wedding bouquet into my hands.*" Jamie paused. "But when you gave it to me, I saw something, something I've held on to all these years."

Trish clasped her hands in front of herself. Vulnerability and uncertainty twisted themselves together in the depths of her chest, pulling the air from her lungs. She didn't know how to respond. Jamie's words were not what she had expected.

"Look, I know we've had our differences."

That was an understatement.

"But it's only a matter of time now . . ."

Trish's stomach knotted. Jamie was gaunt, and her slight frame seemed to quiver with the very effort of standing. Her lips were thin and colorless, her cheeks hollow, but her eyes sparkled with resolve.

". . . and I have something for you . . . a gift." Jamie fumbled with the words.

A gift? Trish cocked her head. Jamie wasn't holding anything.

"My love. It's my gift to you." Jamie's voice broke as tears spilled onto her cheeks. She reached out, enfolded Trish in her arms, then whispered, "I should have done this a long time ago, but . . . I was afraid. Afraid of what you'd think of me. Trish, I'm sorry if I've disappointed you. I know you don't understand me and the things I've done, but please, please forgive me. You're my sister-in-law and, no matter what, I've *always* loved you."

Too stunned to return the embrace, Trish stood speechless. Jamie released her and turned to go back down the front steps.

Trish trembled as the cement-hard wall covering the darkness of her past gave way, crumbling into pieces she was powerless to repair. She felt as though turbulent water rushed beneath her feet, threatening to suck her into a frigid abyss. A memory from another December day surged around the edges of her consciousness.

"Jamie?" The grumbling car lurched into the street. "Jamie!" Trish cried again. The crisp winter rain turned to sleet, and icy droplets peppered her face like small shards of glass.

"Wait! Please! No!" Trish kicked off her shoes and ran down the steps into the driveway. "Please don't go!"

It no longer mattered what the neighbors thought.

The car slid to a stop. Trish knelt on the wet pavement and clutched the rim of the car window when Jamie rolled it down. She grappled with her emotions, finally recovering enough to speak.

"You said you saw something that day at the courthouse. What did you mean?"

Jamie nodded in the direction of the house. "Does all this make you happy?"

"Happy?" Trish was amazed at how strange the expression seemed on her lips. The kind of feelings the word implied seemed foreign and out of reach.

Jamie continued. "My heart told me the bouquet wasn't a pious gesture. You really are a good, caring person, Trish." Jamie looked toward the house again. "Sometimes it just gets lost in the translation."

"Jamie, please come back so we can talk." Awkwardly Trish added, "There must be something else the doctors can try."

"No." Jamie's face was serene. "It's time for me to go."

"Don't say that," Trish said. "You can't mean it. What about Mike and Stephanie?"

The names of her husband and stepdaughter sent a tear down Jamie's cheek. She reached through the window and clasped Trish's hands in hers. Her words were like the feathery white snowflakes that now fell softly from the sky.

"I've had a good life. I've been happy. Everything's going to be okay, Trish. Mike and Stephanie will be taken care of. You'll see."

"Jamie," Trish pleaded. "Tell me—please—what can I do?"

A smile flickered on Jamie's lips. "Give the gift, Trish. Give the gift."

CHAPTER 1

December 20, 2010

TWELVE MONTHS AGO, TRISH INGRAM would have felt immediate disdain for the large manila envelope under the Christmas tree. Twelve months ago, amidst the expensive wreaths, lights, and nutcrackers, she would have considered it a blight on her picture-perfect décor.

But that was then. Now an entire year filled with emotion, turmoil, and resolve had passed.

Like last year, the fragrances of pine and spice drifted on the air, and the music of Kurt Bestor and Josh Groban flowed from the sound system into every room. But there, the similarities between this year and last ended abruptly.

The cookies in the oven were the quick-bake kind from a tube purchased at the grocery store—not those of years past, which had been made with painstaking effort. Trish sat in the same living room on the same camelback sofa with the same Christmas tree glowing in the family room across the hall. It was the only tree she'd put up this year, and the ornamentation on its branches could well be considered sparse. Definitely not the same as last year.

It didn't matter.

She wasn't the same Trish.

After she'd said good-bye to her sister-in-law, Jamie, she'd also said good-bye to a part of herself she could now only barely comprehend: a stranger who'd lived in her home and looked just like her but who had nothing in common with the Trish who now seemed to have arrived at a place of peace with herself and others, even Jamie—especially Jamie.

What a difference twelve months could make.

Last year at this time, there'd been still more to decorate, still more to buy. Much more. It wasn't easy pulling off the model Christmas in Trish's exclusive corner of suburbia, nestled high on the hillside overlooking Utah's Cache Valley. Yet, every year, no matter the cost or trouble involved, right down to her sought-after neighbor gifts and famous gingerbread, Trish had managed to sit atop the pinnacle of local envy.

Touching her fingers to her forehead, she shifted uncomfortably on the couch.

Envy. That's what had been important to her. Back then, she hadn't considered the internal cost for herself and her family—her nearly broken marriage and the alienation of the only child she and her husband, Paul, had, their nineteen-year-old daughter, Sienna. It was the façade, the aura of perfection, that had been paramount in her life—a self-imposed contest wherein she'd hoped to put herself above reproach so that no one could ever accuse her of being less than an ideal wife and mother.

Less than a "perfect" person.

She'd been so steeped in her beliefs that she'd dreaded Jamie's visit last year. *What if her neighbors had noticed?* she'd worried. *What would they think?* Judgments frightened Trish. She had run from them all her life. Now she was embarrassed to think of how she'd judged Jamie. How could she have been so critical of her sister-in-law's actions when she herself had put the lives of her own family in jeopardy?

There had also been the fact that Jamie was dying. In Trish's fairy tale, there was no room for such a thing as death.

The final basis for why she hadn't wanted to see Jamie was complex and frightening. Yet, by facing the truth, she'd learned something important. There had been a reason her life was so out of control. A reason she'd become who she was.

Trish sat upright. This past year had not been easy and, as much fear as she'd overcome, she knew she'd dealt with only a *portion* of the truth. A portion of what she'd labored long and hard to hide from.

Her journey was far from over.

The place of peace where her soul had finally found respite was but a temporary stopping point. Her breathing quickened. She made a conscious effort to slow it and to stem the tide of panic that threatened to overwhelm her. The rest wasn't important, she told herself. She had things under control now. She was on the right track. That was all that mattered.

She looked at her watch. One thirty on the dot. The Monday afternoon was cloudy and overcast, yet her lips pulled into a smile. Soon it would be time to make the drive across town and down the canyon, but first she wanted to collect herself and pray.

Though she'd been raised to believe in God, she couldn't say she'd ever truly felt His steady companionship or love. She had to admit, though, that she'd experienced spiritual sensations now and again, albeit for brief moments. Like unexpected glimpses of shooting stars, she'd initially felt a strong impression that the occurrences were meant just for her, yet they quickly faded and were forgotten. Trish had once liked being independent, liked doing things in her own way and on her own time, and thus had lacked the patience to include any true spiritual elements in her life.

That, too, had changed.

She knelt in front of the sofa and poured out her heart. Not the urgent, demanding kind of prayer she once might have offered, it was a faithful petition for direction interspersed with heartfelt gratitude for Jamie and the gift Jamie had given her last Christmas. *Jamie's gift.*

Without it, Trish would have never been able to make it through this past year or through all the turmoil with Sienna—like the argument they'd had at Thanksgiving when Sienna had vowed never to speak to her again. It was now her turn to give the gift to someone else in need, though she was quite certain they would be as unwilling as she had been to receive it.

Ending her prayer, she pulled herself back onto the edge of the couch. Her hands gripped her knees, and her stomach pulled taut, the muscles feeling like an elastic band forcefully overextended. She tried to chase away the bits of self-doubt that fell on her mind like hot embers. Why, after all she'd done to change her life, were those embers still there? Why did they threaten to ignite a fire of what she feared was unquenchable emotion? She closed her eyes and drew another deep breath. It would be okay—it had to be.

As if in answer to her prayer, a peaceful sensation calmed her. Steadied by it, she stood and walked through the hallway into the family room. She bent and retrieved the manila envelope from beneath the tree, surprised at how bulky and heavy it was. Paul must have left it there for some reason. She turned it over. It was taped shut and bore no clue as to whom it was for, or from. A smaller white envelope, also blank, was taped to the front. Maybe it was something one of the neighbors had dropped off.

Intent on finding a letter opener in the junk drawer, Trish carried it into the kitchen. She rummaged through pens and pencils, small note pads, rolls of masking tape, and other miscellanea; the opener wasn't there. A butter knife would have served just as well, but she decided opening the envelope was not a priority at the moment. She laid it next to the small TV at the end of the counter.

Her thoughts still occupied with what she was going to do that afternoon, she walked to the entryway, pausing just within reach of the doorknob. She smiled as she recalled Jamie's visit. She opened the door. The porch was empty. A few crystals of snow fluttered onto the spot where Jamie had stood for those precious minutes just one year ago.

"Thank you, Jamie," Trish whispered. "Wish me luck."

She locked the door and turned back toward the kitchen. In contrast to Christmases past, the house looked barren. Most of the decorations were still in storage. She'd decided to put up only what she could in a few hours' time, just enough to give the house a bit of cheery holiday radiance. And there were the nativities—displaying them had been important to her.

One, which Trish had received as a child from a friend of her mother, was comprised of small rocks expertly painted to resemble the nativity characters. It sat atop the piano in the family room. Another, crafted in olive wood and given to her by her sister, Ann, occupied the sofa table in the living room. A third nativity, sent by Paul when he'd been out of the country on business during the first

few years of their marriage, had been carved from soapstone. Then
there was the little nativity she'd never before put at the forefront
of her decorating.

Trish moved thoughtfully toward it.

She adjusted the crayon-colored rendition of a construction
paper Mary, moving it closer to the matchbox manger and plastic
Christ child. Sienna had made this nativity in the second grade. In
past years, Trish had relegated it to some obscure corner. Now she
looked upon it with great emotion. In case Sienna came home for
Christmas, and even if she didn't, it held a place of prominence on
the table in the entryway right next to a framed photo of Jamie,
Jamie's stepdaughter, Stephanie, and Stephanie's father, Mike—
Paul's younger brother.

Alongside that photo was one of Paul and Mike standing together
on the banks of the Snake River during a fishing trip they'd taken
several years ago. Trish picked it up, tenderly brushing her fingers
over the image of her husband.

Paul was worlds apart from Mike in both manner and
appearance. Five years Mike's senior, he'd taken after their mother's
side of family. Tall, with broad shoulders and a strong, determined
chin, his hazel eyes were deep-set under a pair of slightly bushy
eyebrows. His mouth was firm, yet a hint of mischief played at
corners of his lips.

Trish traced the image of Paul's lips with her forefinger. How
long had it been since she'd felt their warmth? Unfortunately,
it had been well over a month. Her mind trailed back to the
beginning of their relationship when she was a freshman and he
a senior at Utah State University. She was at once smitten by his
good looks and drawn to his sincerity. Three months after they'd
met, he'd proposed and, after a short engagement, they'd married.
But then Paul's parents and his sister, Louise, had died suddenly
and he'd become swamped with severe depression, not even caring
if he graduated. Determined to keep him afloat, Trish pushed hard,
maybe too hard, she realized now. He did graduate and went on to
reap great success in his career, but the stress of it, in addition to
her unexpected pregnancy with Sienna just six months into the
marriage, made their lives take a particularly difficult track. Things

she should have told him before they were married got shoved aside; she hadn't exactly lied to him—but she hadn't been honest with him, either.

During the ensuing years, they often battled, Paul's easygoing nature frequently pushed to the edge by her passionate temperament. Yet no matter how tough things got, they always seemed to be able to work out their problems—at least up until a month ago. Until her argument with Sienna. Paul hadn't understood, and—bound by the web of deceit she'd spun for years—Trish couldn't explain. Paul began sleeping in the spare room. It was then that their already frayed relationship seemed to unravel like a tattered piece of cloth worn threadbare by the elements.

She sighed heavily, trying to dislodge a burden that refused to be released. Thoughts of Paul's distance were painful to bear. But if everything went according to plan, soon she, Paul, and Sienna would be a family once more. She would prove to both of them that she had changed.

She turned her attention to the other person in the photo she held in her hand. Mike had inherited the physiognomy of his father. His stout body bore a head that was slack jawed under a bushy growth of beard. His face was wide, his complexion uneven. An ample grin betrayed gaps where teeth were missing, and a cigarette dangled from one side of his mouth. He held a ready beer can on the other side.

Whatever force had forged the differences in the brothers' lives and appearances had not diminished the fact they were devoted to one another. A verity that, in the past, had unsettled Trish.

Since before she and Paul were married, she'd made no secret of her objections to Mike, his choices, and lifestyle. At times she'd even gone so far as to urge Paul to stay away from his brother. Her actions had troubled Paul. Even this past year, when she'd tried hard to make her change of heart and attitude evident to him, he still believed she hated his brother. Trish felt a lump rise in her throat. She had never hated Mike. It was just that, like Jamie, Mike was a frightening reminder of things she wanted to keep concealed.

She'd retrieved the fishing photo from where she'd long ago hidden it and displayed it to show her good faith. Had Paul even noticed?

Sadly, after all her years of being the "old" Trish, she knew it was hard for him to buy that she had truly changed, hard for him to trust her. She'd seen it over and over again this past year. They would just get to a point where she thought everything was okay and she could chance revealing her past to him, but then he would pull away. It didn't help that each time he traveled on business—often for weeks at a time—he acted so cautious around her upon his return that it seemed they would have to start all over again, building back up to where they were before he'd left. That wasn't easy. Both their lives were very busy, their schedules hectic. For far too long they'd become accustomed to following a pattern of occupying themselves with only their own concerns.

She'd been on the verge of telling him everything about herself a dozen times, yet one thing kept her from it: fear. And, as in years past, the longer she let things go, the harder it was to convince herself that he would accept her if he knew the truth.

Their relationship had become an awkward match where one of them would try to make things better but the other was too preoccupied, cautious, or, in her case, too fearful to reciprocate.

Back and forth. Back and forth. There was no outcome but misery.

The buzzer on the oven overrode her sense of melancholy. She put the photo back on the table and walked the length of the entryway, then down a short hallway back to the kitchen. She grabbed a pair of oven mitts and pulled the baking sheet from the oven. After placing the hot cookies on a festive red and green plate, she stacked two more platefuls on top and picked up her purse. Shoving the strap over her shoulder, she gripped her car keys in one hand and balanced the plates in the other. The white-chocolate-macadamia-nut cookies were Paul's favorite. The first batch she'd made were for him; she put them in the center of the table in the breakfast nook. As for the plates she held, two were for the kids at The Providence Center in Brigham City.

The other was for Mike.

Her mind raced ahead to that evening. With any luck, after meeting with Mike, she'd have good news to tell Paul. He was due home in a few hours from a midweek business trip. She'd made reservations at Hamiltons, his favorite restaurant, for eight o'clock. Together, they could celebrate a new beginning, and she could devote all her time to stitching her tattered marriage back together and repairing the fragments of her relationship with Sienna.

She switched off the hall and kitchen lights, leaving only the peaceful glow of the Christmas tree. She left the sound system on. The house felt too empty without it. It played one of her favorite recordings of a choir singing "Panis Angelicus."

> *Per tuas semitas*
> *duc nos quo tendimus,*
> *Ad lucem quam inhabitas.*

By your ways, lead us who seek the light in which you dwell, Trish thought as the words filled her with her hope.

The envelope, still unopened, lay next to the TV.

CHAPTER 2

PAUL INGRAM DIDN'T KNOW IF the house felt lonelier when his wife was gone or when she was there. In view of the current state of their relationship, it was a toss-up.

He stood in the kitchen after a coworker dropped him off. It was barely two PM. It appeared as though Trish had left only a short while ago; it was just as well. In the scant flakes of snow on the drive, there was one set of tire tracks leading away from the garage. As usual, Trish was off saving the world or trying to impress someone. He couldn't remember when they'd last spent more than a few seconds together. Speaking only a few awkward, rushed words when they passed each other in the house, they were now so emotionally removed from one another they'd practically become strangers.

His arms ached to hold his wife, but he'd been hurt so many times his heart throbbed in pain. What he intended to do—after weeks of thought on the matter—wasn't going to be easy. He rubbed his forehead as tears pressed at his eyes. He wasn't one to cry, although he didn't find it a bane to his masculinity if he did. His mother had taught him shedding tears was not only acceptable but healthy. Did what he perceive as Trish's frequent inability to cry add to the turmoil that boiled inside her?

He wasn't sure, and he'd run out of time to find out.

After drawing in a deep breath, Paul exhaled in a long, lonely sigh. The house bore the usual Trish-added touches of Christmas pine and spice mingled with the lingering aroma of just-baked cookies. Josh Groban was on the sound system singing "O Come All Ye Faithful." Paul shook his head. He hadn't felt "faithful" in a long time.

He walked to the counter where a still-warm baking sheet bore a few traces of melted white chocolate chips and a couple of macadamia-nut pieces. He picked the morsels off the pan and ate them, scanning the kitchen for a plate containing cookies. Maybe a few left for him?

In years past, Trish had spent hours and hours baking, though he never understood why. She surely didn't derive any pleasure from it—baking made her so irritable he and Sienna had learned to steer clear whenever the oven was on. But then, last year, around the time she usually secluded herself in the kitchen to start making her famous Valentine's Day sugar cookies, he noticed that instead of fussing and fuming with homemade dough, she'd brought home tubes of it from the grocery store.

Somehow, the store-bought dough seemed to improve her baking mood. Paul guessed it enabled her to bake several different varieties of cookies at one time, with less stress. Trish thrived on doing things up big and having a lot to show for her efforts. And, to Paul's amazement, she'd even asked his opinion on his favorite kind of cookie, something she'd never before done in their twenty-plus years of marriage.

His mouth pulled into a weak smile as he picked the last of the morsels off the pan. He'd chosen the white-chocolate-macadamia-nut as his favorite and, after that, when Trish baked, she always made extra for him. That practice had ended on Thanksgiving, though. In fact, Trish had rarely cooked—let alone baked—anything since. The fight they had waged over their daughter's departure seemed to have severed the already strained ties of their relationship. Today, seeing the cookie sheet made Paul hope that maybe . . .

Laying his black leather jacket on the counter, Paul thrust his hands into the pockets of his jeans and walked into the family room. Thoughts of his life with Trish played out like a depressing movie on the screen of his mind. The last year seemed to start out with a glimmer of promise. Something about Trish had softened, giving him reason to think there might be hope for their future together. But the year was now about to grind to a rocky end, devoid of anything but despair.

He moved in close to the Christmas tree. Bearing only a fraction of the usual ornaments, it looked almost timid. He ran his fingers across the "needles" on one of the artificial branches. He'd tried to understand what the jagged pieces of his life had splintered into. He'd tried to understand Trish. But the more he tried, the more hazy and muddled everything became.

Ever since they'd met, Trish had been the epicenter of an emotional earthquake that had rocked his life.

Not all of it had been bad.

The sensations he'd experienced when he'd first looked into her brown eyes—eyes that were as deep and mysterious as anything he'd ever tried to comprehend—had captivated him. It was Trish who, after the untimely death of his parents and sister in a plane crash, had pushed him to finish college. She'd urged him to see his dreams to fruition. He felt she'd believed in him.

A powerhouse of determination, she'd prodded him to avail himself of any and all opportunities to move up the ladder of success, to always go the extra mile, to work as much overtime as possible. She'd even planned and hosted elaborate parties for his superiors and coworkers. Thanks in part to her persistence, he'd risen quickly from a green, newly married student to an executive raking in a six-figure income at E-Quip, a large manufacturing firm.

For a time, having so much money seemed glamorous. They dined at exclusive restaurants, traveled to the best destinations. But five years into it he began to feel suffocated. His job as a research executive kept him cloistered in an office, and the hours he put in were exhausting. He liked hard work, but he preferred to deal directly with the public, promoting E-Quip's line of outdoor equipment and accessories. That would have meant a big cut in pay and a house the fraction of the size of this one. He didn't care if they lived in a humble home instead of this vast "hotel." Trish did; she wouldn't hear of him switching jobs. It was then that Paul had begun to wonder if what she really wanted was for him to succeed, or if she just wanted all the money his success ensured.

He turned away from the tree and went to the hall closet, where he pulled out his snow boots and winter parka. In the laundry room, he grabbed a few pairs of clean jeans and socks. For the last two weeks, he'd been gathering his things and removing them from the house. Had Trish even noticed? If she had, did she even care?

Next to the door that led out to the garage, Paul threw everything into a pile and then went back down the hallway and up the stairs. In the master bedroom, he pulled a large duffel bag off the top shelf of his closet. From one of the drawers in his nightstand he retrieved the watch Trish had given him on their tenth anniversary along with a few letters she'd written him while they were still dating. One of their wedding photos sat on top of the armoire. He took it down and tucked it under his left arm, deliberately not looking at it as he did so.

On impulse, Paul leaned over and picked up Trish's pillow. He'd been away on business so much lately that he didn't remember when he'd last slept in their bed. He pushed his face into the pillow, breathing in Trish's scent. After a moment, he lowered it back onto the bed and patted it into place.

Back in hallway he paused, leaning against the railing that opened to the family room below. Was there anything he'd forgotten? There wasn't one single spot in the entire house that felt welcome and homey. The place reminded him of a museum with dozens of invisible Do Not Touch signs. The furniture, artwork, and various antiques were worth a mint, yet they weren't important to him—Trish could have it all.

He put the duffel on the long table next to the railing, set the wedding photo on top, and rubbed the back of his hand across his eyes. The figures of Trish and him dressed in their wedding clothes, young and full of promise, stared up at him and sent a tremor of anguish through his soul. If he'd known on their wedding day that things were going to end up this way, would he still have married her?

Yes. No question.

The good times they'd shared, though too few and far between, had enriched him beyond measure. There'd been his family's beach house on the Oregon coast that they used to stay at during the summers when Sienna was little. Ski trips to the Alps—Zermatt, the mountain village at the foot of the Matterhorn with its horse-drawn sleighs—and Italy and Germany, where he and Trish had shared anniversaries away from the demands of home and work.

Those memories were priceless—not so much the places as their time spent together.

Trish could be so loving, which made it all the harder when she was not; the thought of life without her was unfathomable. But the thought of life with her was as well. He had to concentrate on Sienna, help her pick up the pieces of her life.

Turning the photo over and placing it among the other items in the bag, Paul realized there were several questions to which he might never have answers. Had Trish ever really loved him? What had happened in her life to harden her?

He started slowly back down the stairs. What had allowed him to endure so long in the marriage was the hope that one day she'd see they'd reached the pinnacle and stop striving for more, stop being so materialistic, and then just start living life, loving him again like he believed she had when they were first married. Yet, even when it was obvious they had more than most people could ever aspire for in a lifetime, she still hadn't been content. She had to stay one step ahead of everyone else.

Why had that been so important to her?

Always worried that some obscure neighbor or acquaintance might have something better, she not only insisted on possessing the latest name-brand styles in clothing, but she also cycled through all the rooms in the house, decorating them with her lavish tastes until they were so overstocked with expensive items they were uncomfortable to enter. Then, within only a matter of months, she'd become disillusioned with what she'd done and would want to start all over again. Why wasn't she ever satisfied? Why couldn't he and Sienna make her happy?

Paul pressed his right hand to his chest, trying to relieve the dull ache that had taken up residence there. He was tired of feeling this way. Life was too short, and the kind of existence he and Trish had fallen into wasn't living.

He packed up his pile of clothing and arranged everything around the photo so it would be protected during his trip to Sienna's apartment, where he planned to stay at least temporarily. He stepped into the garage and hauled the duffel bag over to his Harley, the motorcycle Trish hated so much. If only she had let him explain . . .

Would she have understood even then?

The bike lent him freedom away from the persistent demands of his job and, besides Sienna, his group of riding buddies were his only family. And, of course, Mike, who was often too drunk to even function—Trish would be the first to point that out. Trish thought the bike meant he didn't want to spend time with her, but that wasn't so. The Harley had simply filled a void in his life that Trish, these past years, didn't seem to notice was there.

A few moments later, he found himself back for one last look at the Christmas tree. Beneath it, on the lace tree skirt, there were only a few presents. In his hands, Paul held a small blue velvet box adorned with a silver ribbon. He crouched down and placed it under the tree. With his arms resting on his knees, he studied the package. How many guys left their wife a Christmas present under such circumstances?

In his heart, he felt it was right.

Looking at his watch, he saw it was nearly three. Why did part of him still want her to come through the door? It wasn't going to happen. She probably wouldn't be back for hours and, really, it was just as well. He placed his finger on a branch of the tree, a sort of farewell gesture to an old friend who seemed as sad and downtrodden as he was. It wasn't likely either of them would witness any joy this Christmas.

There was a large manila envelope next to the TV on the kitchen counter. Paul glanced at it, but it didn't have a name or an address on it.

Must be Trish's, he thought as he switched off the Christmas music. Silence permeated the house, smothering him with a disturbing sense of finality. Through the windows by the breakfast nook he saw that the clouds had knit together outside, darkening the sky, another winter storm no doubt on its way.

As he prepared to leave, by habit born from years of living there, he looked down the hall through the entryway and made a visual check to see if the front door was locked. His gaze passed over the table in the entry. Recognition fluttering like a butterfly taking wing, he moved toward the table with deliberate steps. Next to a little paper nativity was a certain photograph. A photograph of him and Mike on a fishing trip to the Snake River. Paul hadn't seen the picture in years. As much as Trish loathed his brother, he assumed she'd thrown it out. But here it was—framed and on the table.

Why?

CHAPTER 3

"SO, I PRESS THE NUMBER eight how many times?"

"Once. See, that makes a T. Then press the seven three times for an R, the four three times for an I. Then press seven four times for S, and then four two times for an H. Wow. You've almost got it." Anika Marks watched Trish fumble with the keypad on her cell phone. Texting was not her strong suit, but with the fourteen year old's help, she soon typed out two short sentences.

This is Trish. Please call me. "Wow, indeed. Good thing it's not an emergency. I'd really be in trouble." Trish stood next to the teen in the hallway outside the office of the Providence Center, where she had just dropped off the two plates of cookies.

"You're getting faster at texting, Trish—kind of."

Like all the kids at the Providence Center, Anika had endured her share of tough times. When Trish started volunteering at the center in February, Anika was sullen and withdrawn. But over the past several months, she had blossomed into a cheerful, outgoing teen with many friends, despite her life in a foster home where she'd been placed after being taken from her drug-dependent parents.

"One more thing." Anika reached for the cell phone and punched more buttons. "Okay, when it rings, it won't really ring—it'll be a song, 'Jingle Bells,' and it's sung by chickens."

"Chickens? I didn't know chickens could sing."

"I guess they kind of cluck to the tune. Now, remember what I showed you last week? When it's me calling, it will show a paintbrush. Since her last name is Hart, when Carrie calls, there'll be a pink heart. Your husband is the motorcycle, and Lexie is the barking dog—that's all you had left, except for the cat, and you know Lexie isn't wild about cats. I could put that on for your daughter, if you want."

Trish didn't want to acknowledge that there was no need. Sienna never called.

She changed the subject. "How's the painting going?"

"Come and look."

Trish followed Anika across the hall to the art room. On an easel near a window stood a large canvas which bore a near-finished painting of Santa sitting in his sleigh.

"I'm almost done. I want to work on his beard a little more, and I need to finish his clothes."

Trish admired the brilliant strokes of red which filled in the lines of Santa's suit. The shadows and highlights Anika had applied made it look like real velvet.

"Anika, this is wonderful. I love how you've painted his suit, and his eyes—so wise yet merry—they sparkle. You've truly captured his spirit."

Trish looked at more of Anika's finished canvases. One depicted an old Indian woman in a blue shawl, her hands busy at a loom, weaving a blanket. There was a child with a puppy and a portrait of a boy. Each piece was striking. The girl definitely had talent.

"Anika," Lexie Rogers called from the hallway, "time for computer lab. Kelsey and Tanisha are already in there."

Lexie, the director of the Providence Center, had arranged for Anika to be tutored in art in exchange for her promise to help the younger kids hone their computer skills.

"See you at practice?" asked Trish.

Anika nodded and smiled. "Hope you enjoy the chickens."

"Um, yeah, chickens. One of these days, remind me to tell you about my chicken horror stories."

Lexie joined Trish next to the Santa painting. "Anika's really doing great," she commented after the girl left the room.

"Without a doubt. It's always amazing how far a little belief in these kids will go."

"Thanks to you, Trish. You're the one who came up with the idea of having Mrs. Cantwell tutor her. It's been great for them both. Anika has tremendous talent—she just needed some direction—and now Mrs. Cantwell doesn't feel so isolated after her retirement. And once Anika began to believe in herself, she was able to reach out and help the others." Lexie held up a section of newspaper. "Hey, listen to this."

Children from the Providence Center, a local after-school program for kids ages seven through fifteen, will take part in the annual community Christmas program at the Brigham City Tabernacle, Tuesday, December 21, at 7 PM. As part of the program, the children will perform an original song they have written entitled, "Goodwill Toward Men," which is based on true stories of acts of kindness and generosity.

Under the supervision of volunteer mentors at the center, the children spent several weeks looking for stories about people helping one another. One story involved a boy in Canada who raised money to help build a school in a third-world country. Another was about a group of children from Brooklyn who, despite their own poverty, held a fundraising event to help cover the medical bills of a child in another state who needed life-saving surgery. One of their favorite accounts was about a young girl suffering from a rare, incurable disease who decided to sell most of her own possessions to raise money for a burn unit at a children's hospital.

"That was cool," said Derrick Gant, a thirteen-year-old, who faced time in detention for vandalism before becoming involved with the Providence Center. "Most people, they think the stuff you have is important. This girl didn't want to be like everybody else. She wanted to make a difference. What she did made us think about what we could do."

"I'll tell you I never thought I'd hear something like that coming from Derrick." Lexie looked over the top of the newspaper and grinned at Trish before she continued reading.

That kids like Derrick were able to undertake the project and then, with the help of conductor and local high school music teacher, Nate Cook, put their thoughts into words and set those words to music, is a tribute to the center's founder, the late Jamie Ingram. Thanks to

Mrs. Ingram, who saw the need for a program to help at-risk kids use their time after school in a productive manner, these children now have an opportunity to express themselves and contribute to the community in a positive manner. A few years ago, most of them would never have imagined they would even care to be involved in such a way.

"Jamie didn't want just a place for kids to hang out after school so they could stay out of trouble," says Anika Marks, who admits she was once involved with gangs. "She taught us we had value. Most of us thought we didn't. At the Providence Center, we're not just friends, we're family," the teen added.

Anika, a gifted artist, is just one of the center's many success stories. Several of her paintings will be featured as part of a slide show—created by another teen at the center, fifteen-year-old Carrie Hart—that will be shown when the kids sing their song at the program.

Lexie looked over the top of the paper a second time, nodding her head. "Here's the best part."

Both Anika and Carrie are quick to credit volunteer mentor, Trish Ingram, sister-in-law of the late Jamie Ingram, for their involvement in the local holiday celebration. "Trish is wonderful. She helps us find opportunities to see who we can become."

As in years past, local celebrity soprano, Lynette Campion, will be a featured guest soloist. Campion says she's excited the kids will be involved and looks forward to . . .

Trish cleared her throat and grimaced.

"You really don't like that woman, do you?" asked Lexie.

Trish squared her shoulders and looked away, past Anika's painted Santa and out the large windows of the art room to where a few flakes of snow had begun to fall. "Let's just say Lynette is one of those people who it's better to love from a distance."

Lexie laughed and folded the newspaper in half. "How did you manage to convince her to give up one of her numbers so the kids could take a few minutes before their song and tell what they're thankful for?"

"It was Mr. Cook. He has more of a say than Lynette would like to think he has. I just attended a couple of the planning meetings. Lynette wouldn't even give me the time of day."

"Did you know her before you went to the meetings?"

Trish shifted uncomfortably from one foot to another. The answer to Lexie's question was simple yet achingly complex. She and Lynette had met when they were girls, but the association had quickly become painful "Yes," she finally said, "but that's ancient history. What matters is that the kids are so excited. In just over twenty-four hours they'll be performing for the public for the first time."

"Trish, all the things we've been able to be part of this year are a tribute to you as well as Jamie. After her death, you jumped in and really got things rolling."

Warmth flooded into Trish's face and neck. She hadn't become involved with the center in order to seek praise or recognition, and she didn't feel she deserved it now. "I can't take any credit, Lexie. It all belongs to Jamie. She rallied the leaders of the organizations in town and got them involved. It's just grown from there. The music room remodel, the computer lab with all its hardware and software, even the new furnace we're getting, those are all things Jamie had in the works before she died."

Trish and Lexie walked back out into the hallway, the length of which was covered with a brightly colored mural the kids had painted to depict their dreams. While some sections bore mere stick figures and others showed varying degrees of skill, the mural conveyed vibrant messages of hope. Anika painted herself as an artist sitting at a canvas. Carrie was a veterinarian. Ten-year-old Kelsey, who had been emotionally-abused, painted herself as a doctor. Aaron had used strong colors to show himself being drug free, unlike his father. Others had created images of themselves riding bikes, skateboarding, or dancing. Their painted figures had one thing in common: they were smiling—untroubled—unlike the real-life versions of themselves who were subject to depression and frustration.

"This mural was part of Jamie's genius," Trish said. "A way to teach them they could choose something better and make the most of their lives. Something they could see every day they were here. I wish I'd had something like this when I was a kid." She walked the length of the mural. "They've come a long way. I'm so proud of them."

"You've come a long way as well, Trish." Lexie touched her arm gently. "Jamie would be proud of you. Don't sell yourself short. You've helped bridge economic and ethnic barriers, selling the idea of this place to the movers and shakers who've gotten us the grants we needed. These kids now have some great opportunities. They're learning about leadership, unity, respect, and empowerment. You've helped teach them they can choose to react positively to their challenges."

"Creep!"

A voice interrupted Lexie.

"Loser!"

"And . . . most of the time they remember." Lexie chuckled in response to the sound of an argument in the homework room. "If you'll see to that, I can hear the phone ringing in the office. Maybe it's the man about the furnace. The grinding of the old one is making me crazy."

"Oh—Lexie," called Trish after her, "have you seen Carrie today?"

"No. I was hoping you had . . . Talk to you in a minute."

"Mrs. Ingram, Kelsey thinks I'm stupid!" said eight-year-old Brent Davis.

"Brent, I never said that. I told you to work on your handwriting. How do you expect me to help you with spelling if I can't read what you write?"

"You hate me!" Brent spat.

"Don't put words in my mouth. I'm trying to help."

"Kelsey, would you mind going to make sure things are running smoothly with the food pantry project?" Trish smiled at the girl. "We need to have everything packed into boxes for tomorrow . . . I need a minute with Brent.

"What? Are you going to tell me I'm stupid too?" The boy wadded up a piece of paper and put his head down on the table where he'd been working. His body shook.

"Kiddo, I don't think you're stupid at all." Trish slid into a chair next to him.

"Kelsey does. She thinks she's high and mighty because she's a mentor and she can boss everybody around."

"Kelsey has worked hard to earn her position as mentor."

"Yeah, whatever. What does she know about anything? She has no idea what it's like to be stupid and worthless."

The child's words tugged at Trish's heart. "Can I tell you a story?" she asked.

"I don't care." Brent groaned.

Trish crossed her arms and rested her elbows on the table. Sifting through her thoughts for the right words, she leaned toward the boy. "Once there was a girl not much older than you. She thought she was stupid and worthless too. Some people actually told her she was—but most didn't. She just assumed everyone felt the same as the mean people who told her bad things.

"Some days she wanted to crawl into a corner and hide. You see, she didn't have parents—that is, her parents were . . . gone." Trish lifted her hand to her temple, and her fingers brushed back a few strands of her hair. "She lived with other people. They were good to her, but she couldn't see it at the time. She was angry with everybody, mostly herself. Among other things, she thought she was somehow to blame for her parents not being around."

Brent lifted his head to look at her. "Was she?"

Trish hesitated and put her hands, palms down, on the table before replying. "No."

"What happened then?"

"Well, she grew up and still felt like she wanted to hide. Big people can't hide as easily as kids, so she did *other* things."

"Like what?"

"Well," Trish forced a smile, pulled a quick breath in, and let it out through her mouth. "She spent too much money and tried to make everyone think she was perfect. The harder she tried, the more miserable she became, and the more miserable those around her became."

Brent looked at her expectantly.

Trish issued a short cough. "But she found out there was a better way. She found out there were other people who struggled in life. Not all of them thought they were stupid and worthless, but they . . . Brent, have you ever heard the saying, 'Be kind, for everyone you meet is fighting a hard battle'"?

The boy shook his head.

"Plato was a Greek philosopher—a very smart man—he's the one who first said that. He lived a long, long time ago, yet he knew what he was talking about. It's just like you and Kelsey. She might seem like she has everything going for her and that she's trying to be bossy. But it's because she has fought and is still fighting a hard battle that she cares so much about you. Maybe she doesn't show it the way you think she should, but every day she tries to help you with homework. She could be somewhere else, but she *chooses* to be with you."

"Mrs. Ingram, what battle is Kelsey fighting?"

"Ask her, Brent. Talking to people and learning about who they really are is much better than judging them for who you think they are."

A tall girl with curly black hair appeared in the doorway. "Hey, Mrs. Ingram, great cookies. Oops, sorry to interrupt. What time is practice?"

"Five."

"Thanks!"

"You'll be there, right?" Trish asked Brent.

"Yeah." The boy nodded. "I'll be there."

"Good." She tousled the child's hair before she pushed the chair back from the table and stood up. "Now go get a cookie before they're all gone."

In the hallway, a group of kids crowded around her.

"Are the people you told me about still coming tomorrow night?" asked Anika.

"Yes, they are."

"Do you really think they'll like my art?"

"I do. And they can tell you about their school."

"You know my foster parents could never pay . . ."

"It's all right. These guys want to give you full tuition. And since the school is only thirty minutes away, you can attend classes there during the day. Mrs. Cantwell is going to help you get some release time from school."

"And I can still come here afternoons?"

"You bet." Trish hugged the girl firmly. "You bet. I'll see you in awhile, okay? I've got to go talk to Lexie."

In the office, Lexie looked concerned. "Trish, you said you hadn't talked to Carrie Hart today. When was the last time you did?"

"She called here last Thursday to say she wasn't feeling well; she had a sore throat and hadn't been at school. I really should have tried to phone her this morning to see if things were okay." Trish looked at her watch. "I have an errand, but afterward I'll stop by her brother's apartment to see how she is and if she needs a ride to practice."

"That might be good, because—"

Kylee Andress burst in. "Mrs. Rogers, I've got the skill surveys done you wanted me to do. Guess what? Everybody wants Derrick to teach us how to longboard. Won't that be fun? You and Mrs. Ingram can come too."

Trish looked at Lexie and laughed. "Sure, if you have one that has brakes. Right, Lexie?"

Seemingly oblivious to the comment, Lexie picked up the phone and began pressing numbers.

"Be back in two hours," said Trish.

CHAPTER 4

TINY FLAKES OF CRYSTALLINE SNOW fell as Trish drove away from the Providence Center and pulled her silver Mazda Miata onto Highway 89. She drove south one mile before turning off to the west on a narrow stretch of pavement. Two inches of frosty white snow had left a soft, fluffy layer on the gravel lane leading to Mike's small redbrick house. Deciding to park on the street by his battered mailbox, she walked the few hundred yards down the lane, the soft crunch of her shoes the only noise in the otherwise quiet afternoon.

In the distance, a wispy curl of smoke rose from the chimney of the stately old two-story farmhouse her grandparents, Herman and Lily McClure, had built following their marriage in 1932. In 1980, when they'd built a more modern home a short distance away and retired, Trish's parents, John and Kate McClure, had brought their family back to Utah from Colorado and moved in. Trish, her sister, Ann, and brother, Robert, lived in the house from the time Trish was thirteen until she married. Robert had also married and moved to Salt Lake. Now, with John and Kate in Omaha, Nebraska, serving a mission for their church, Ann and her family lived in the farmhouse, the third generation of McClures to watch over the home and the precious peach orchards surrounding it.

Thoughts of her sister evoked a sharp feeling of concern that caused a tingling sensation in Trish's arms. She and Ann hadn't exactly seen things eye to eye for a long time. She brushed the feeling aside. First things first. She had to deal with Mike; later she'd phone Ann and see if they could arrange a family Christmas get-together on the weekend.

Trish slowly mounted the three concrete steps that rose to meet Mike's worn wooden porch. Grandpa McClure had built the home for the migrant families who helped tend the acres of peach trees during the summer and harvest the fruit in early fall.

With only the slightest hesitation, Trish knocked on the wooden screen door. No answer. She studied the once-ornate woodwork around the top of the porch. The wood was sagging and weathered from countless winters. Pieces of it hung in sad disrepair.

Nearly eight years ago, her father had offered to rent the home to Mike for a ridiculously low sum. Trish was astonished at the time, believing her father to be foolhardy. Sure, Mike had had a family—his first wife, Liz, and three-year-old Stephanie—but how was practically giving him the house going to help, she'd wondered. Mike was an alcoholic and couldn't seem to keep a job for more than a few weeks at a time. If he would just kick his drinking habit and get to work, there'd be no need for handouts.

She shook her head at the thought of her own coldness.

The old screen door creaked open as she tugged on the handle. She knocked on the interior door. A groan sounded deep within the house, undoubtedly human. Trish steeled herself. Just as she reached up to knock again, a bearded man in a dirty T-shirt opened the door a few inches. Mike. He grunted a sort of cynical laugh, planted his left hand high on the door frame, and leaned his head against it.

"Slumming, aren't you, Trish?"

In the past, she'd tried to look beyond his disheveled exterior—the missing teeth and the ever-present smell of alcohol and tobacco—to try and see something of the goodness that existed in her own husband. Mike and Paul were, after all, brothers. Sometimes she'd been successful in seeing the best in Mike. Most of the time, though, she had not.

Now, however, it didn't seem to take so much effort—the exteriors most people constructed were often a stark contrast to what lay beneath. Just as it'd been with her, pain often hammered the nails into a façade meant to hide and protect vulnerabilities—supposed or real.

"Hi, Mike," she said warmly, ignoring his demeanor. "How are you?"

"How am I?" He snorted then coughed, running a hand through his long, oily hair. The smell of alcohol washed over her. "How am I? Well, let's see, I haven't had a decent meal in over a week, the power company is coming right after Christmas to turn the lights off, my boss laid me off until February, and the state thinks I can't take care of my kid. Of course, Liz, my beloved ex-wife, is running around in another state and could care less if the kid is dead or alive. Oh, and did I forget?" He belched. "I've also got one dead kid and one dead wife. But that's good news for you, isn't it? Less presents to buy, right? So you tell me how I am." He pointed a rough, grimy finger at her.

Trish didn't break eye contact. "Can I come in?"

He motioned dramatically, ushering her inside. "Make it quick, okay?" He shot a hand toward a dusty television set in the corner. "I've got things to do."

Trish walked over several items of dirty clothing and a variety of cans and bottles. She found a semi clear place next to a large wooden table and sat down on a plastic chair, holding Mike's plate of cookies in her lap.

"Is Paul . . . okay?" Mike remained standing a few feet from the door. The note of concern in his voice convinced Trish that a soft heart beat underneath the gruffness.

"Yes, Paul's fine. Thank you for asking. He'd be here, but he, uh . . . he had to complete some business out of town before the holidays. He should be back later this afternoon."

The statement was a half-truth. Paul was out of town on business and was due back this afternoon. And surely he would have been here with her—had he known she was going to pay Mike a visit. What she'd omitted was the fact that he had no idea she *was* going to talk to Mike and, certainly, no idea of her intentions.

"Okay," Mike said as he nodded absently.

Trish held out the cookies. "Here, I made these for you."

Mike grunted again and accepted them. "Thanks. They're good," he mumbled as he took a bite.

"Mike." Trish shifted on the chair and crossed her legs, trying to appear calm and casual. "How's Stephanie doing with her grandparents?"

"Okay." Mike nodded again. "She's okay with them. Doing pretty good in school . . . just got this card." Mike stepped to the table, put the cookies down, and retrieved a homemade Christmas card from the top of a stack of bills. Inside the folded red construction paper, a picture of eight-year-old Stephanie smiled amid an assortment of Christmas stickers. Mike's face softened.

"*Merry Christmas. Love you, Dad. Hugs and kisses, Steph,*" he read.

"That's nice. She's such a great kid." Trish paused. "This must be a hard time of year for her, especially being away from you and . . . with her mom gone and now Jamie gone too. Losing two mothers, well, I just can't imagine how hard that would be."

"What's your angle, Trish?" Any trace of tenderness in Mike melted like snow on a hot, sunny day. "You don't bother with anything unless you have an angle—an angle that suits Trish McClure Ingram." He pointed an accusatory finger, his face growing red.

"Mike," Trish said, folding her arms in front of her. "I'll get to the point—my angle, if you choose to call it that. Your in-laws are getting old. I know they love Stephanie, but they've got their hands full. She's an active girl. At her age, she needs more. Mike, she needs a mother."

Mike kicked a pile of cans across the room. "And just who do you have in mind, Trish?"

"Me," Trish said with determination.

"No." Mike kicked more cans aside then grabbed a chair and planted it firmly in front of Trish, throwing himself down into it. Defiant and angry, his eyes met hers. "It ain't gonna happen, Trish. No way. You're the last person on earth I'd let her live with. So why don't you just pack up your little bag of pity and good intentions and hit the road." His face inches from hers, Mike gestured wildly toward the door.

Keeping her composure, Trish picked up the card and looked at the photo of Stephanie. "I know you want what's best for her. I know you care—"

"Care? You gonna lecture me about caring? You McClures think you've got it all figured out. Think you're all high and mighty, lookin' down on everyone else."

Trish bit her tongue. "No, we . . . I . . . don't think I've got it all figured out. I'm just talking as one parent to another here."

"One parent to another, huh? What in the world do you know about being a parent? Do you even know where Sienna is? Didn't she move out six months ago? Have you even talked to her since Thanksgiving? At least I know where my kid is." Mike's fist hit his chest.

Trish swallowed hard. "Sienna is . . . attending college in Ogden. She's living in an apartment there."

"An apartment, huh? And where will Stephanie get dumped when you get tired of her?"

Trish closed her eyes and tried not to cry. "Look, Mike, I wasn't tired of Sienna. She's nineteen years old and free to come and go as she pleases. At Thanksgiving we . . . we had a misunderstanding . . . we . . ."

"Why don't you just admit it, Trish? Sienna has been last on your list for a long time. She didn't measure up to be a big-deal McClure like her mother, so she was expendable."

Tears filled Trish's eyes and spilled onto her cheeks. A big-deal McClure? Not hardly. Mike was way off target. Though she called John and Kate McClure her parents and they'd legally adopted her as one of their own, biologically, she was not their daughter—a secret she'd guarded fiercely throughout her life. And Sienna . . . expendable? Her stomach knotted. She pressed her hands, palms together, at her lips as she tried to suppress the pain that tore at her heart.

A few moments later, after silently measuring her next statement, she tried a more gentle tone. "Look, Mike, say what you will about me—but it's unfair to drag the McClure name into things." She wanted to say *after all John McClure has done for you,* but she resisted. "The McClure family is a good, decent family. It's me who's to blame. And you're wrong about Sienna. I love her. Granted I've made lots of mistakes, but I want very much to repair my relationship with her."

Mike gave her a curious stare and sat back in his chair.

Trish continued, emotion pulsing through her tone. "I know you'll probably never understand, but when Paul and I married, I was determined to make my *family* proud, to be the best . . . McClure." She used the name for clarification even though Mike obviously had no idea of her true parentage. "To be the best McClure yet. And to be someone Paul could be proud of." She felt the blood rise up in her cheeks along with a surge of multifaceted shame. She fought hard to quell it before she could continue.

"Somewhere along the line my good intentions got mixed up with notions I had about being the perfect wife and mother. Life became a very personal, competitive battle. People around me would say, 'Oh, Trish, your house is so beautiful, you're so good at decorating, so good at this and that, you're the best.' It felt good to have that kind of recognition. But as time went on, I had to do more and more, be better and better, to get the compliments. The years passed and, before I realized it, both Sienna and Paul were so far away from me I didn't know how to get them back."

Trish's breath came faster. "I didn't realize until it was almost too late that people were what mattered—not things. Surely you can understand . . ." How could she explain how she felt without offending him? What was it she had told Brent about talking to people, about understanding? *Plato.* She started again. "Mike, it can't have been easy for you. The shock of losing your parents and sister in the plane crash, the divorce from Liz, yours and Jamie's baby, Victoria, being stillborn, and then Jamie. It's true, I've judged you harshly in the past. I didn't understand. I'd like to think I do now. I want you to know how very sorry I am for the way I once acted. I realize now that people do things for reasons other people don't understand." Trish's voice dropped to a whisper. "Things even they don't understand." Her body quivered as she waited for Mike's response.

He crossed his arms tightly across his chest. "Yes. Yes, that's true," he mumbled. "But what I don't understand is what all this has to do with Stephanie. You barely even know her."

"Do you remember when Liz had Stephanie and they came to stay at our house for a few days until Liz got on her feet?" Mike didn't respond, but Trish went on. "I remember holding Stephanie and rocking her to sleep; she was so tiny and had all that beautiful black hair. I sat in my grandmother's rocking chair and sang, 'I Am a Child of God'. . . ." Trish's voice broke. "I promised her if she ever needed anything . . . if she ever needed *anything*, I would be there for her."

"So, now you think she needs a mother?" Mike leaned forward.

Trish looked at her hands then rose and walked toward the window. Outside, the snow had increased to a near blizzard, covering everything with a deep quilt of icy white. Her words fell softly like the snow. "Did you know Jamie came to talk to me one year ago today?"

"Jamie?" Mike asked, his voice low and reverent. Trish knew Mike had dearly loved his second wife. But she hadn't known how much until this moment when his whole countenance seemed to change at the mere mention of her name. "Jamie," he whispered. "What did she say, Trish?"

"She told me she that was going to die, that she accepted it, and that she wanted to say good-bye."

Mike smiled. "She never told me she came to see you . . . but that would be something she'd do, even if . . ."

"Even if I never treated her very well?" Trish finished his sentence. "You're right. I never understood her, either. I made judgments. I was wrong." A sob caught in her throat. Tears stung her eyes. "There was something else." She turned back to Mike. "Jamie gave me a gift—a gift that changed my life and made me see just how selfish and self-centered I was. Mike, I came here to ask your forgiveness for everything I've done in the past and because I want to give Jamie's gift to you—and to Stephanie."

"Gift? What do you mean?"

"I can still see her standing there on the front porch." Trish pressed her fingertips to her lips for a moment before continuing. "She was so nervous yet so determined. She told me she had a gift for me. Being the kind of person I was then, I remember looking down at her hands for some wrapped present. There was nothing. I thought, *What on earth is Jamie talking about? A gift?* She looked straight at me with those beautiful sky blue eyes of hers and said, 'My love. It's my gift to you.'"

Tears flowed freely down Trish's cheeks now. "Can you believe it, Mike? Me—me of all people? She wanted to give me her love—that was her gift. I'd never thought of love as a gift, but Jamie, oh, Jamie, of course *she* would."

"What happened then, Trish?" Mike stood up next to his chair, his eyes moist.

Trish shared the rest of what Jamie had said and how something had broken loose inside her as she listened to Jamie that day. But Trish carefully avoided telling Mike the full extent of everything she'd experienced.

"I was so ashamed for all the callous things I'd ever said to her and to you, ashamed about how pious and shallow I'd been just because you and Jamie were different from Paul and me. I suddenly realized all the troubles the two of you had—money, alcohol, Victoria's dying. Jamie's cancer. Jamie never once—never once—felt sorry for herself. She lived and died with tolerance and grace. Mike, she was truly an angel. But I don't have to tell you that, do I?"

Trish stepped through the clutter on the floor to Mike's side. "I'm so grateful for Jamie's gift, Mike. It changed my life. I'd been looking for something, and I didn't even know it. Something money could never buy—Jamie gave it to me."

Mike jerked his head up. He stood and reached out for Trish. His hand fell back to his side as though he didn't quite know how to complete the gesture of tenderness. "Trish, I'm sorry . . . I don't know what to say."

"I just want you to think about it. I'd like Stephanie to come live with us, if you agree, even for awhile. She'll be closer to you than she is with your ex's parents in California, and you can come see her anytime you like. I made her a promise a long time ago, and I want to keep it. I'm at the Providence Center most afternoons now, and knowing how much she loved it there . . . I know it won't be the same for her without Jamie, but I think she'd enjoy being a part of things again. The kids miss her so much."

"Lexie told me you've done a lot of good there, Trish. Jamie would be thankful. And you're right. Stephanie did love it there, loved helping the other kids. This other thing, her living with you and Paul. I think it might be okay. I would like to see her more often. I would like her to be closer than California. I want to be a part of her life," he looked down at the beer cans at his feet, "as much as possible. I'm working on doing better. Until then, she does need a mother . . ."

"Mike, you have my promise we'll take very good care of her. I know I can never fill Jamie's shoes but, hopefully, I can at least be a special aunt, someone she can turn to, someone who will love her. I want to give her Jamie's gift."

Trish reached out and embraced Mike. He didn't resist. "And I want to give it to you, too. I do love you, Mike. Say you'll give me a chance . . ."

Mike hadn't shut the front door, and unexpectedly a handful of snow fluttered inside as the old screen door rasped wide open on its hinges, then snapped shut. Mike and Trish looked at one another, then made their way across the room. Outside, they saw the screen door had brushed a broad imprint in the new-fallen snow drifting across the porch—wide enough for someone to pass through. From the door, to the edge of the porch near the steps that led to the short sidewalk and gravel lane beyond, six distinct footprints were impressed into the snow. The stairs, walk, and lane were unmarked.

Trish suddenly felt an overwhelming and unmistakable sense of peace. Somehow she knew that things would work out because what she was doing was right.

Mike turned to Trish, tears on his cheeks, and nodded.

CHAPTER 5

1966

HOT PINK, WHITE, PURPLE, TEAL, brown, and orange miniskirts bobbed up and down around the dance hall. There were flowered miniskirts, polka-dot miniskirts, and even miniskirts that looked like plastic. All the girls wore them except Cecile Anderson who, once she reached the top of the stairs and saw miniskirts and go-go boots, started back down the way she'd come up.

"Hey, Poodle Skirt. You're in the wrong place, aren't you?" chimed a girl running up the stairs past her.

"Maybe the wrong decade." Another laughed.

She pushed against a tide of teenagers anxious to join in the throng that moved to the beat of the Beach Boys. Their big hit from last year, "Help Me, Rhonda," throbbed in her ears. At the bottom of the stairs, she turned toward the front door. Two girls she knew from high school walked in with dates. She ducked into the coat closet. After they walked past, she decided on another escape route: the back door.

Just a few steps down a hallway, a shortcut across the snack area, past the restrooms, and she'd be free. It was a good plan—except the door wouldn't open.

"Sorry, we keep that locked this time of night."

Cecile whirled around. A boy she remembered from her art class stood holding a bag of hot dog buns. He was dressed in a snack bar uniform—black slacks, white shirt, and paper hat.

"Don't look so scared. I'm not after you. I just had to come back to the storeroom for these."

Trying to avoid direct eye contact, Cecile looked from the bag he held in one hand to the crutch he gripped in the other, then at his leg, which was bandaged from the knee down.

"Land mine," he said. When she gasped, he added, "Hey, I still have my leg. It's just a scratch. Doc Crandall says I'll be good as new by fall. Then I'll be going back."

"Back . . . where?"

"You been hiding somewhere, girl?" He looked her up and down.

Cecile glanced at her skirt then tried to push past him, inadvertently knocking the buns out of his hand.

"My leg!" he cried as she picked up the bag and shoved it back at him.

"I didn't touch your leg. Now look out."

"Hey, I'm just jokin'."

She wanted to tell him it wasn't funny, but as she looked into his face and took in his brown eyes and the way he smiled at her, a pleasant kind of warmth flooded through her. She pushed the feeling aside.

"Look, I might not have the money to dress like those girls upstairs, but it doesn't mean you can harass me."

"Harass you? You mean what I said about my leg? Ah, come on. I do that to everyone. It had nothin' to do with you."

"I . . . I'm sorry then. And sorry about the bag, I didn't mean to knock it out of your hand. I just need to get out of here."

"Here—hold these for a minute and I'll unlock the door. Are you sure you wanna go?"

"Can't you see? I wore the wrong thing. They're all making fun of me."

"They *all* made of fun of you?"

"Well, some girls on the stairs."

"Did you know them?"

"Not personally." She looked down at the floor. "But I got the point. I don't belong here."

"Who says?"

Cecile grabbed the side of her skirt and shook it so he could see the poodle. "Where have *you* been hiding?"

"Oh." His face turned red.

"Now, please let me out."

"I'd like to, but it looks like I left the keys by the cash register. Stay here a minute. I'll be right back." He returned a few seconds later, turned the key in the lock, and pushed open the door. "Hey, I think you look mighty pretty. Why don't you let me get you a soda?"

"Thank you, but I can't. Good night."

As soon as the door closed behind her, she was sorry. He'd only been trying to be nice. But coming here had been a mistake. She reached into the pocket of her skirt for the key to her brother-in-law, John's, old Chevy pickup. It wasn't there. She walked back to the door and pounded on it.

"Okay, already. I'm comin'." He swung the door open and looked at her, surprise evident on his face. "Hey, why are you back?"

"My truck key—I must have dropped it." She scanned the carpet inside. It wasn't there.

"You drive a truck? I'm impressed."

"It's not mine. It's my brother-in-law's. He's letting me drive it for a while." She retraced her steps through the snack area toward the hallway and then back again. She stopped short and took a deep breath.

The young man smiled. "Looks like neither of us can keep track of our keys tonight. You want me to go look for it?"

"Would you, please?"

"Sure. But only if you'll let me buy you a soda. What'll it be?"

Cecile looked around. There were only three couples in the room, and none of them seemed to be paying any attention to her. "Okay. Sprite."

"Good choice. Be right back."

She seated herself on a stool and looked into the mirror on the wall behind the soda fountain. She tried to poof up her hair with her fingertips, but it was no use. She'd need a can of hair spray to make it stay in place, and hair spray was a luxury she couldn't afford.

Upstairs, she could hear the Mamas and the Papas' "California Dreamin'." Things quieted down for the slow dance.

"This it?" He walked out of the hallway and placed it in her hand.

"Yes, thanks. Where was it?"

"On the stairs. Took me a minute to find it, though, under everyone's shoes. Roxy's gonna play some stuff by the Stones tonight. That's why they're flocked up there like pigeons."

"Roxy?"

"Yeah, she owns this place. She's a friend of my uncle's. She'd like to marry him, but he won't have anything to do with it."

"Why? Doesn't he like her?"

"No. Nothin' like that." He turned to the soda fountain and then put a glass of Sprite on the counter. "It's just, well, things in our family haven't always been the best. That, and he drinks a bit—sometimes quite a bit."

Cecile sipped at the Sprite. "He's an . . ."

"It's okay to say it, pretty girl. Yes, he's an alcoholic. Learned it from his dad, my granddad, they say. But that's okay. When I get back I'm going to take care of him, get him sobered up. Roxy might have a husband yet."

"Where are you going? You said you were going back somewhere?"

"Vietnam. Sorry, I guess in my Mr. Snack Bar duds you wouldn't recognize me. Navy Third Class Petty Officer Clark." He made a mock salute.

"Wait a minute." She clinked her glass down a little too hard, disappointed that this handsome young man appeared to have lied to her. "You said your leg had been hurt by a land mine. Last time I checked, there weren't any land mines at sea."

Just then, the girls she'd passed earlier walked in. Their faces took on looks of disdain; then they started to giggle. "Nice skirt, Cecile. Guess as often as you get out, you didn't know the styles have changed."

Even with his crutch, the boy behind the counter made it to a spot between Cecile and the girls in no time flat. "Hey, ladies. Didn't anyone tell you tonight is Fifties Night? Why, it looks like Cecile here is the only one who can read the posters. Looks like she'll win the contest. Maybe you two ought to go home and change."

Between them, the girls issued a nervous grunt before one asked, "Really?"

"Yeah, hurry and go change before Roxy puts on the Chuck Berry and Chubby Checkers stuff."

Cecile covered a smile with her hand as the girls rushed from the room. "That wasn't very nice."

"Neither was what they said to you."

"They were right. I have no business being here. I just was . . . lonely, and I heard about the dance. I just turned nineteen—I graduated last month. Most of the kids here aren't any older than fifteen or sixteen. Kids my age go to the dances at the college."

"I'm here—I just turned twenty."

"This is where you work. You're supposed to be here."

"Yeah, well if it wasn't for this leg I'd take you to one of those college dances, pretty girl."

"You mean your leg that was nearly blown off by a wave of water?"

"Okay, it wasn't a land mine. But I did get hurt on duty—seriously. One of the officer's guns fired on accident. The bullet ricocheted off a wall and hit me in the leg. I promise. It's just hard to explain, and people kind of look at you like you're makin' it up, even when it's the honest truth. The land-mine thing, that's more or less a joke for those who stare."

"I didn't mean to stare."

"Neither did I."

"What do you mean?"

"At you. At your eyes. They're about the prettiest eyes I've ever seen. I mean it."

Warmth flooded back into Cecile. "Thank you." She picked her key up from the counter and slid off the stool. "I really need to go."

"You haven't finished your soda. Why don't you stay and talk awhile."

She gestured toward the hallway. "They'll be back. Besides . . ."

"Besides what?"

She twisted her key around between her fingers. "Why do you want to talk to me?"

"You mean why do I want to talk to the girl everybody says was responsible for what happened to her sister? The girl whose mother everybody says hates her?"

Shocked by his direct manner, she felt her cheeks flush hot. Halfway to the back door, she heard his footsteps as he hobbled after her. He put a hand on her shoulder.

"I don't care what anybody says, Cecile Anderson. I know you weren't to blame for anything."

CHAPTER 6

December 2010

IT TOOK NEARLY AN HOUR for the snowplows to carve a path through the fresh-fallen snow. Trish left Mike's just after four and drove the still slush-covered roads to the grocery store where she picked up ingredients for several holiday meals. Everything she'd bought would stay cold enough in the car while she went to the hour-long practice at five. Then she'd have to hurry to get back over the canyon in order to put things away and be ready in time for the eight o'clock dinner reservations she'd made at Hamiltons. Her heart skipped a beat. She could hardly wait to see Paul.

As the checker scanned her purchases and then waited for the lengthy receipt to print out, the tone on Trish's phone sounded with a chicken chorus clucking out "Jingle Bells." The screen showed a barking dog.

"Hello?"

"Trish? This is Lexie."

"Hi. I know. I'm not sure how she did it, but Anika set my phone up so that it plays 'Jingle Bells' while a—"

"Trish, listen. I just got a call from the police."

"The police?" Trish adjusted the bags of groceries in her cart and thanked the checker. "What's going on?"

"It's Carrie. She hasn't been in school. Mrs. Gunderson, her homeroom teacher, is worried—Carrie was crying when she left class last Wednesday. The school couldn't reach her on her cell or at her brother's apartment. Carrie didn't have a locker partner, but one of the other girls knew the combination. She decided to look inside. Trish, there was an entry in one of her notebooks . . . The school contacted the police because they think it's a suicide note."

Suicide.

Wheeling the cart out of the store, the word echoed cold and harsh inside Trish's head, pricking her senses and making her feel short of breath. Determined to keep her emotions under control, she stuck out her chin and tried to push the word from her mind.

"Trish? Are you there?"

"What did it say?"

"I don't know. They're on their way over here now. They called first to give me a heads-up. They didn't want to alarm the rest of the kids. I've sent everyone home. I told the kids I had something important come up. I told them not to come back until the practice at five. Maybe by then we'll know more, although I have no idea what to tell them if . . ."

As Trish deposited several quarters into a red metal bucket, a Salvation Army Santa with an obviously artificial beard clanged a hand bell and wished her a Merry Christmas. Returning the sentiment, she entered the parking lot and fixed her gaze on her Miata parked at the far end of the lot. The cart slid sideways, its hard black plastic wheels resisting little piles of slush formed on the asphalt by the car tires of numerous holiday shoppers. With one hand she clutched the phone. She still hadn't responded to Lexie. With the other hand, she clutched the bar of the cart and maneuvered around patches of ice. A loud honk sounded and she pulled up short.

"Trish, what on earth is going on?" Lexie asked.

The driver of the car, an older woman, shouted something, but the remark seemed to be whisked away by the chill wind that swelled suddenly, heralding yet another episode of winter weather. Tiny flakes swirled around Trish like confetti as she pushed the cart, fighting the wind as well as the turmoil that swelled within her.

Suicide.

She'd tried to make a point of keeping busy these past several days—busy enough that the word and all its inherent implications were relegated to the far reaches of her mind. Even before Lexie's call, the word had threatened to overtake her, as it had each day of her life for as long as she could remember, no matter where she was or what she was doing.

Today's date, December 20, marked one year since Jamie's visit.

"*Trish?* Are you there?"

In the past week, she'd made numerous visits to friends and neighbors, attended the Christmas party at the nursing home where she volunteered, and, Saturday, had overseen Snow Day at the Providence Center. She'd been so busy she'd almost been able to keep the word at bay . . . almost like when she used to go to excesses in decorating or shopping. Almost like she used to when she tried to pull off the perfect image so no one would ever suspect anything about her past.

She'd deliberately planned the trip to Mike's today—on this date—for two reasons: she wanted to honor Jamie, and she wanted to try to forge a good memory to help erase the scars of the past.

Now, with the trip to Mike's and grocery shopping over—the only two tasks she'd scheduled besides practice—it looked like she might make it through the day itself and have a good, positive memory as well.

But that had changed.

Here the word was again, assailing her and accompanied by even more fearsome implications than she could ever imagine. Was this date fated for tragedy?

"Carrie . . ." she cried out, but the name was swept away by another word.

Suicide.

With each step, the word thundered louder and louder in Trish's head. She pushed the cart with savage abandon, ignoring the icy slush and trying to focus on her schedule for the rest of the week: *Tomorrow, Tuesday, 10 AM: help the elderly at the nursing home wrap presents, make cards, and read Christmas books; 2 PM, do the same things at the Providence Center; 4 PM, help Lexie take the kids to the food pantry to deliver the food they had been working to collect; 6 PM, arrive at the old Brigham City Tabernacle to make certain everything was in place for the community Christmas program at seven.*

She had things to do, people to call, and . . .

"Trish. *Answer me!*" Lexie insisted.

Flushed and out of breath, Trish shoved the cart toward her car. It slid into the back bumper of the Miata, leaving a small dent. She grabbed her keys from her purse. They slid from her cold, fumbling fingers and clattered noisily on the ground. She bent to retrieve them. Standing up, she was overcome with a sudden rush of trepidation that nearly swept her off balance. A dark, angry tide threatened to smother her.

"Trish!" Lexie sounded frantic.

At last gaining entrance to the trunk, she roughly shoved the groceries inside, not caring where she put the bread, rolls, or eggs. She'd probably regret that later. For now, all she could think about was transferring the white plastic bags into the trunk as quickly as possible.

Managing to bring herself out of shock for just a moment, she realized that Lexie must be wondering if she were crazy. "I'll call you back," was all she could manage to say before she disconnected. She shoved the phone into her purse and slammed the trunk, leaving the cart where it had slid to a stop. She jammed the key into the driver's side door, jerked it open, and fell onto the seat. The key slipped into the ignition, but she lacked the strength to turn it. As if to protect herself from her own fears, the heel of her left hand roughly pounded the button that locked the Miata's doors.

Seizing the steering wheel with both hands, she slumped forward. Why was this happening? She had tried so hard to help Carrie. Tried so hard to put her own life in order. Things had turned out better than she'd expected with Mike. He was going to allow her a chance with Stephanie. She felt she had gained a chance to redeem a lost part of herself. A chance to give Jamie's gift in a very special, personal way, prove her good intentions to Paul, and start over again.

Jamie.

Trish's heart fluttered. The impressions she'd experienced at Mike's gave her reason to hope for good things . . . but something was wrong.

Still so very wrong.

She was trying to prove to herself—to God, to everyone, that she'd changed. She really wanted to. Why must she be continually scorched by the burning embers always smoldering just beneath the surface of her psyche? Why didn't she have the power to extinguish them? Why didn't she have the power to help Carrie? She'd thought she had the answers; she thought she and Carrie had connected—Carrie with her blond curls and sparkling blue eyes, so full of promise and so ready to take on the world.

"No!"

The knuckles of her hands white from the force with which she held the steering wheel, Trish's shoulders heaved, and her breathing became jagged and raspy. Her body shook. At times she'd been able to pretend that the Trish whose life had been marred by the word *suicide* was a different person living a different life, a life the regular, everyday Trish could pick up and put down at will, like a photo of someone else. But this—this was inconceivable. Had there been warning signs with Carrie? Signs she had ignored while pretending she was some sort of saint?

A knock sounded on the passenger-side window. Trish roughly swiped her fingers across her cheeks, wiping away tears and droplets of melted snow. Reflexively, she checked her appearance in the rearview mirror. Her hair matted with melted snow, her makeup blotched, she was a mess. Self-conscious, she glanced over to see who'd knocked.

A young woman wearing a long white coat stooped down, looking at her through the window. She held a strand of her straight auburn colored hair away from her face and mouthed the words, "Are you okay?"

Trish nodded stiffly. The woman gave her a quizzical look. To convince the woman, Trish started the car and forced a smile and a friendly wave. Driving slowly from the lot, she glanced back at the rearview mirror. The woman stood in the same place amidst the blowing snow, watching her departure.

A lump formed in Trish's throat. Oh, if it could only be as easy as saying, "No, I'm not okay. Please help me!" But she could never say something like that to a complete stranger. She could never admit her own failings. She wasn't the type to open up, not even with her own family. Not even with Paul—especially not Paul.

When she reached the highway, her fingers tightened on the steering wheel until they were nearly numb. Her thoughts vacillated between the parts of her life that were fact and fiction, parts that were engaged in a dangerous duel. As far as Trish could see, it was a battle with no winner and everything to lose.

She pressed her foot hard on the Miata's accelerator. A thick fog of anguish descended on her already clouded mind. She couldn't go back to the Providence Center and face the police. She maneuvered the car onto a stretch of highway leading to her sister's house. She had to talk to someone. Maybe Ann was home. Her foot still heavy on the gas pedal, the car picked up speed. The flakes of snow were larger now, soft and full like feathers. She switched the wipers on to clear the windshield. She drove straight into the blizzard, only vaguely aware of the Sinclair station she'd sped past on her right and an orange and white image that was the closed-for-the-winter burger joint.

Here and there, small orchards dotted with now-barren fruit trees flowed together in her peripheral vision. In less than a mile, she would again pass the lane that led to Mike's house. In a mile and a half, she'd pass the old wooden fruit stand where, as a child, she'd peddled peaches during the heyday of the area known as Utah's famous fruit belt.

West of the fruit stand lay hundreds of acres of peach trees—one of the oldest orchards in the state—stretching north and south and sandwiched in between the boundaries of I-15 on the west and Highway 89 on the east, orchards owned by the McClure family.

Twilight began to fall and, with it, additional pinpricks of anxiety that pierced Trish's already fragile state of mind. She tried to push thoughts of Carrie further and further away. Who did she think she was? She'd once told herself she could control everything in her life down to the most minute detail. But grim reality had just manifested itself. The fact remained that her life was marked by numerous elements that were out of her control. Though she was trying to remedy it, literally every relationship she had was in jeopardy. She was a stranger in both her immediate and extended families—a wanderer in a foreign land with no knowledge of the emotional language that might help her to survive. And now . . . *Oh, Carrie!*

The sensation of rushing water surrounded her. She recognized with a cold terror she'd experienced too many times before the feeling of not being able to find or draw air—the feeling of drowning. She felt completely helpless, like her body had been pulled down into the depths of a dark, frigid river. Would she have the strength to propel herself back to the surface?

She banged her hand on the steering wheel and shook her head. She would find something—anything—and hang on to it with all her might.

As hard as she tried, there was nothing to grasp.

She looked at the clock on the dash of the Miata: 4:27. The wipers worked furiously, brushing a thick layer of snow from the windshield. Suddenly, ahead of her, a set of taillights flashed a bright red warning. In three successive bursts of brightness, the illumination broke through the surreal state enveloping her and replaced it with a raw, rigid fear. She applied the brakes, but the car was traveling much too fast for the conditions.

Trish didn't realize how slick the road had become.

CHAPTER 7

WHAT PROMPTED HER TO LIGHTLY tap the brakes of her red Honda Accord, Sienna Ingram didn't know. But the impression to do so was as loud and clear as if it had been spoken to her from the backseat of the car. She whipped her head around to see if someone was sitting there. Of course not. But what was going on? A shiver rippled through her upper body. Was someone trying to tell her she was in danger?

Though she'd felt compelled to tap the brakes three times, she hadn't felt like she needed to slow down. On the contrary, she felt she needed to keep up the speed she'd been traveling at, albeit a slow and steady one, in the blizzard. She probably should have started back to her apartment sooner, before the bulk of the storm hit.

The late afternoon was bitter cold, even inside the car. Sputtering occasionally, the Honda's heater wasn't functioning properly. Only now and again did a small blast of warmth seem to burst forth from one of the vents. Her job as a cashier at a gift shop a few miles from where she attended college at Weber State University barely paid for gas and food. Repairs on the car were out of the question. She knew her dad would help, but he'd had so much going on in his life lately, she hadn't wanted to trouble him. Knots formed in her stomach. The relationship between her parents wasn't good—she wished she could make it better, but she'd learned from experience that she couldn't.

It had been a relief to move out on her own last summer.

For as long as she could remember, her parents' house had never felt particularly homey. Sadly, her father had discovered the same thing. For the past couple of weeks, between his business obligations, he'd been moving a few things at a time into her apartment, where he planned on staying until he could find a place of his own. He'd been at the house early that afternoon—dropped off by a coworker—to get the rest of his belongings and his Harley. Sienna knew because she had been there right before him to pick up a few Christmas ornaments. He'd called her cell to say he was on his way over, but she'd had to leave before he arrived. She was on her way to visit someone. She told him she'd see him later.

Yesterday, she'd stopped by the house and left something for her mother. Sienna held the steering wheel tighter. When Grandma Kate had called from Omaha yesterday morning, they agreed it was up to her mother to work things out on her own—but would she?

Shifting forward in her seat, Sienna strained to look through the windshield. The wipers beat back and forth across it in dull, heavy thumps. Her heart beat with a much faster rhythm. She hated driving in the snow.

The person she'd visited was an old friend of her grandmother's, Bessie Clark. No matter what her mother elected to do, Sienna needed to move forward with her own life, to move herself away from the secrets that had mired her family for years. And, she'd needed someone to talk to—she hadn't realized how very much she'd needed that. She bit her lower lip. It wasn't as though, in the past several years, she'd had a mother to turn to, and, after her Aunt Jamie had died, she'd felt more lonely than ever.

She and Bessie had formed a quick bond. Bessie, with her easy manner and heartfelt sincerity—Sienna loved her completely.

After their visit, Sienna had passed back through Brigham City and continued south on Highway 89, where the snow now seemed to blow almost sideways, whipping against the car and making it difficult to see the road.

She shivered again. There was absolutely no heat coming from the heater now. Her coat kept her fairly warm, but her gloves were in the backseat. She didn't dare take her hands off the steering wheel to get them.

The highway was empty—no other vehicles in sight. Driving became more complicated. It was as though she were trying to maneuver the car over thick foam padding. Since the lines on pavement weren't visible, she could only depend on the faint tracks left by another vehicle.

She thought of her father. He'd probably left the area hours ago. She hoped he was back—safe in her apartment. As soon as she could, she'd call him on her cell. Right now she had to keep her attention on the road.

Fear pricked her skin like dozens of tiny needles. Her chin was almost on the steering wheel, her body leaning forward in an attempt to give her eyes some advantage. It was no good. The blowing snow filled in the tire tracks she'd been following.

"Aunt Jamie?" Sienna's voice was low and shaky. Before Aunt Jamie died, she told Sienna she'd only be a whisper away. Sienna had talked out loud to her dead aunt before. Even when her desperate mind demanded it, Aunt Jamie never spoke back to her, but Sienna felt peaceful sensations. Impressions that she wasn't alone.

Sienna needed those feelings now more than ever.

"Aunt Jamie. I'm scared. I can't even see to turn around and go back. I . . . I don't know where I am."

For a moment, the tire tracks seemed to return. At least a foot away from where the Honda was traveling, they stretched on for a short distance ahead. Sienna steered toward them, desperation causing her to jerk the wheel too hard to the right. The car slid across the road and suddenly dipped downward, a hard bump bringing it to a stop.

***

THE REAR END OF THE Miata veered toward the right. Things happened so quickly Trish forgot to lightly pump the brakes; she forgot the maxim her old driver's ed teacher and Paul had repeatedly tried to instill in her: steer into the slide.

Trish braced herself as the car spiraled into a sharp circle. At any moment, she expected to hit the car in front of her—the car whose taillights she'd seen.

The Miata slid through yet another forward half circle before coming to stop sideways in the road. Before the stop, Trish closed her eyes, a self-protective measure for what she felt was an imminent impact. Now she opened them and looked up.

Though the snow blew and swirled around the car, she could see for a few yards in every direction. There were no other cars in sight, only dozens and dozens of mule deer running across the highway, just feet away from her.

Trish blew a long, ragged breath of air through her tightly pursed lips. If it hadn't been for the taillights of the other driver—a warning in the blizzard—she would have been in big trouble. If she had hit the deer, the impact would have totaled the car.

For a moment, she sat still and silent. She'd avoided a collision, but everything in her life felt like it was still spiraling out of control. Talking to Ann wasn't going to help. Ann had never understood anything about her life. Ann was a McClure—Trish wasn't. It was that simple, and that complicated. In trying to convince herself to go to Ann's, she'd only been running—like she had all her life. Running and hiding. Hadn't she told Brent just hours earlier that you couldn't hide when you were an adult?

Fanned by the near accident, the embers burning her soul turned to hot coals. No matter what she did—no matter how hard she tried, there was constant tribulation; things never seemed to get any easier. She knew she had to take responsibility. She had to return to the Providence Center and face the police.

After the remainder of the herd crossed the road, she pressed the gas pedal and inched forward, turning the car around.

***

WHERE WAS SIENNA? PAUL PACED back and forth in the small living room of her apartment. He'd tried her cell a dozen times. No answer. Outside it was a whiteout; the news said it was moving south. Was Sienna caught in it? She'd said she was going to visit someone. Why hadn't he asked who or where?

He grabbed the wedding photo from the duffel bag and sat on the couch, staring at it. How he needed Trish now. How he wished things had never reached this point. Had he been wrong to leave? He ran things over and over in his mind. He'd been desperate; he hadn't known what else to do. There were so many things that didn't make sense. His efforts to understand what was going on were only met with opposition from Trish.

Things with her were so very impossible.

When he picked up his cell phone, his thumb hovered over the numbers that would connect him to Trish. He clenched his teeth. Given the current state of Trish's relationship with their daughter, would she have any idea where Sienna was? He hit the number two. The speed dial for home. The phone rang and rang with no answer. He punched the number three, Trish's cell—no answer. That morning, when he'd been so certain leaving was the right thing to do, he'd blocked both numbers from being able to call him—he hadn't wanted an argument with Trish over his decision. Now she wouldn't be able to reach him if she tried. He'd have to keep trying to call her. *What if Trish is caught in the storm?* he thought.

His heart felt like it stopped. He realized he was just as worried about Trish as he was Sienna. He held the picture to his chest for moment then looked down at it. "I do love you, Trish. I love you with all my heart . . . even if it's broken."

Phone in hand, Paul resumed his pacing. At the side of Sienna's small television set was a stack of DVDs. Killing time, he read through the titles until he came to one marked "Angelfish Summers." Several years ago Trish had arranged for all their old 8-millimeter videos to be put on DVD. Sienna must have taken this one when she'd moved out. He switched on the television and found the remotes for both it and the DVD player. Forwarding the disc to the section entitled "1996," he sat down on the couch

"Mommy, Mommy, look—a starfish!" Sienna was just five-years-old.

"It's beautiful, honey. See if you and Daddy can find another one. Oh, look over there on the side of the rock by the purple anemone. There's a great big orange one."

Paul switched off the DVD then got up and walked to the kitchen. It was too hard to watch the happy scenes on the Oregon Coast from summers long past. He opened the fridge and took out the mayo and some lunch meat. He hadn't eaten all day. He found the bread in a drawer and yanked a plate from one of the shelves. He picked up a butter knife from the drain board and put everything on the table. Halfway through making a sandwich, he realized that no matter how difficult it was, he *had* to watch the DVD.

"Look, Sienna. Look at all those big barnacles."

"They look funny, Mommy, like there are baby birds inside sticking out their beaks and trying to talk to us." Sienna laughed. *Trish laughed too.*

The sound washed over Paul, leaving him with a fierce longing to hear it again. The next scene on the DVD was in the kitchen at his parents' beach house—Angelfish Lodge—near Depoe Bay. He and Mike and their sister, Louise, had spent summers there with their parents. When his parents and Louise had died, the ownership of the house had fallen to him and Mike.

"Tell us what you're doing, Mommy," he heard himself say playfully.

"I'm fixing breakfast for my family." Trish winked as she held out *a plateful of food.*

"And tell us, gorgeous Chef Mommy, what's on the menu."

"Eggs, bacon, and waffles."

"Um, too bad."

"Too bad? Don't you like my waffles?"

"Yeah, but I was hoping you were on the menu, too." Paul growled and moved in for a kiss. Trish laughed again and started to tickle him. Sienna joined in the fun.

As he sat on the couch, Paul didn't realize that tears were running down his face until he felt the dampness and wiped it away.

After Sienna was born, it was important to him to take his family to the beach house as often as he could. He loved Angelfish Lodge and wanted his family—Trish and Sienna—to have good memories of it as well. From the time Sienna was five until she was almost twelve, they'd spent a good portion of each summer there riding bikes, crabbing and clamming, and visiting all the lighthouses. Lots of days, they simply hung out on the beach enjoying each other's company.

Enjoying each other's company.

That had felt *so* good. For reasons Paul never understood, Trish was always relaxed when they were on the coast—relaxed and happy. As much as he did, she loved the beach house and how his mother had decorated it. She never bothered to change a thing. It was as if she could just live—and laugh—and not worry about impressing anyone or keeping up with the Joneses. She never opened up and laughed anywhere else but there.

"Wave to Mommy, Sienna." Trish was filming again. Sienna was riding her little pink and purple bike down the hard edge of the sand on the beach. Seagulls flew up around her. The sky was so blue Paul felt as if he were right there again, with the warmth of the sun shining down on what they all thought at the time was a never-ending summer. On the television screen he watched himself run after his daughter, gently teasing her.

"I'm gonna beat you. I'm faster than you!"

"No." Sienna giggled. "No, you're not, Daddy. I'm faster. Race you to that log."

"Thank you," Trish had whispered, the recorder picking up her soft voice. "Thank you, Heavenly Father, for my family. I love them so much. I'm so thankful for them. Please always take care of them, watch over them, and keep them safe. I couldn't bear to lose them . . ."

The screen went blank. The scene was over. Paul cried openly and knelt down.

It had been too long since he'd prayed.

CHAPTER 8

TRISH FOLLOWED A SNOWPLOW BACK to town. The storm seemed to be moving off in a different direction. Stepping from her car into the parking lot of the Providence Center, she could hear the kids singing—practice was well underway. A single police car was parked near the door.

She stamped the snow off her shoes in the foyer. Her chest seemed to constrict. She felt the urge to turn and run back outside. Apparently hearing the sound of the door, Lexie emerged from the music room.

"Trish? Where have you been? We've all been worried sick. I thought something had happened to you too."

"I'm all right, Lexie," Trish said, even though she wasn't. "Are the kids okay?"

"They're fine. They decided to go on with practice—they felt that would be what Carrie would want."

"Any word?" Trish managed to croak.

"Nothing. Here, come into the office. Detective Jorgenson is going through some of Carrie's things from the locker she has here."

A tall, middle-aged policeman rose from a chair and greeted Trish. "You must be Mrs. Ingram. I'm glad you're here." He nodded toward Lexie. "Mrs. Rogers was very worried."

"I'm so sorry, the storm and all . . . Lexie said there was a note. Can I see it?"

"At this point, no. It's considered evidence. But I can tell you what it said. The girl indicated she couldn't go on, that things were just too difficult, and that she was giving up."

"That's all?"

"That was it. I'm sorry, Mrs. Ingram. I understand you and the girl were very close."

Trish put a hand to her forehead. "That's what I thought. Obviously I wasn't as much help to her as I'd hoped. I can't say that I'm not to blame for this."

Lexie stepped forward. "You've been a good friend to her. She looked up to you."

"I don't know why, Lexie. What did she have to look up to?"

"Mrs. Ingram, when was the last time you spoke with her?"

"Last Thursday. I was here Thursday—midafternoon—doing paperwork. She phoned to say she wasn't feeling well. I asked what was wrong. She said she had a sore throat. I should have known it was something more. She's prone to depression."

"But she's been okay for a long time, Trish." Lexie jumped in. "You couldn't have known. It's been months since she was in trouble. Months since she's been anything but happy."

"Sometimes people can look fine on the outside and still be hurting so bad on the inside they can barely cope." By the look on Lexie's face, Trish knew she'd spoken with more force than she'd intended. She directed her next comment to the detective. "What about her brother? You have spoken with him, haven't you? When did he last see Carrie?"

"We haven't been able to locate the brother, either. His coworkers at the gas station where he's employed said he hasn't been in to work since last Wednesday. But they say that's not uncommon, that his job was on the line because it's a regular thing for him not to show up."

"That's true," Trish said. "He's not the most dependable person. I don't know why the state allowed him to be her guardian in the first place."

"Mrs. Ingram, if the girl was in school last Wednesday, when she evidently left the note, and you spoke to her Thursday afternoon and she was okay, she's most likely just gone off somewhere with her brother."

"No, she wouldn't do that. Their relationship is strained. She's trying hard not to be like him."

Lexie jumped in again. "Mrs. Gunderson thought it was a suicide note, Trish. But Officer Jorgenson thinks what Carrie referred to in the notebook was the fact that she wanted to quit school, that it was too difficult for her."

Trish's hands flew into the air. "She's been working so hard, Lexie. She wouldn't jeopardize her graduation next spring."

"Like you just said, people can be hurting so bad that no one else—"

Trish cut her off. "I know that's what I said, but I really don't think she would ditch school for no reason. What if it is a suicide note? What's being done to find her?"

"Mrs. Ingram," said the officer, "the girl has a long criminal record. She's been picked up numerous times for theft and shoplifting. Kids like that, you just don't know what they'll do. She's probably run away."

"Kids like that? What do you mean?"

"Like Mrs. Rogers just said, you yourself pointed out that—"

"Forget what I said, okay? I was talking about . . . myself—not Carrie. I have to believe in her."

"With all due respect," the detective said, "you're contradicting yourself. On one hand you're acknowledging she could be depressed and nobody would know it—even that she's prone to depression. And you implied you think it may have been a suicide note. But now you're saying she wouldn't quit school and that you have to believe in her. I'm confused. Which is it?"

"Look," Trish asserted, "let's just find her. Don't you have men out searching? Look at the weather." She gestured out the office window. "She could need help!"

"I need to ask you to calm down, Mrs. Ingram. And, no, we're not out looking for her."

"*Why?*"

"With her background and her brother gone as well, like I said, the girl probably wanted to quit school, and she and the brother have gone off somewhere together, maybe to see a relative for Christmas."

"But you don't know that."

"No, but I won't send anyone out to search until we have a reason. I'm listing her as a runaway—nothing more."

"She doesn't have any relatives to go to." Trish could feel her pulse pounding in her head. "That she's missing should be reason enough for you to start a search."

"Trish, please lower your voice. Let's not upset the kids."

"I can't believe this." Trish put her face in her hands.

From the doorway came a voice. "Mrs. Ingram, are you fighting a hard battle?" It was Brent.

"Brent, I'm sorry. I shouldn't be talking so loud."

"It's okay. Whatever is wrong, just talk to the person—"

"I can't," Trish interrupted the boy. "Carrie isn't here. Some things just can't be fixed, Brent."

"Trish!" Lexie's tone was a stern reprimand. "Brent doesn't need to hear that."

"You're right." Trish looked from Lexie to Brent and then to the other kids gathering in the hallway. "I'm sorry," she said, sobbing as she ran past them out the front door. *"I'm sorry!"*

***

A LEFT TURN, THEN A right, took Trish into the cul-de-sac where her home was situated at the far side of the circle. The drive through the canyon had left her feeling stressed—the road conditions had been horrible. The conversation with the officer had made her angry. It didn't matter what kind of life Carrie had lived; she was still a human being—just a teenage girl. They should be out looking for her. Trish had contemplated searching herself, but with the roads the way they were, she knew she had to have help.

Paul.

He and his biker buddies had helped search for missing children before. He should be home by now. He would know what to do. Some of the men in the group were lawyers, one a retired highway patrolman. Surely they could convince Detective Jorgenson that a search for Carrie needed to be initiated. She'd tried several times to reach Carrie on her cell phone, to no avail. As soon as she got the groceries inside, she'd try again.

To her dismay, Trish saw that the long, steep drive leading up to the house hadn't been shoveled. She'd told Kevin, the neighborhood teen who usually did the drive and walks, that Paul would be home that afternoon and would remove the snow himself with his snow blower. But Paul obviously hadn't been home yet. When she'd left at one thirty for Mike's, the snow had been barely two inches high. Now over six inches lay heavily in the drive, undisturbed by any mark or evidence of tire tracks.

Where was Paul?

There was no sense in even trying to get the Miata up to the garage. It would only get stuck. So after parking and accidentally grinding the rims of the tires on the cement curb, Trish struggled up the driveway in the deep snow, her arms full of groceries. Her shoes quickly became uncomfortably cold and wet. And, oh, why in the world couldn't she have remembered to open one of the home's three garage doors with the control before she'd gotten out of the car?

A thin layer of ice had formed at the base of the snow. Twice, she nearly slipped and fell. Managing to get to the garage door nearest the front of the house, she clumsily balanced the groceries as she punched the security code into the control box.

A few seconds later, the door went up and Trish walked into the dark garage. She'd held out a faint hope that Paul *was* home, his tire tracks perhaps indiscernible in the snow on the drive.

The garage was empty.

A feeling of foreboding spread through her like a shot of anesthetic, rendering her uneasy on her feet. Fumbling again with the groceries, this time dropping a jar of parmesan cheese, she unlocked the door leading into the kitchen. Two bags balanced on her left knee, the handles of an additional two slung over her right arm, she pushed open the door with her shoulder. Three more bags remained in the trunk of the Miata. They would have to wait.

She lugged the groceries down a long hallway, past the downstairs guest bathroom on her right and the laundry room on her left. Arriving in the kitchen, she dumped the bags onto the large island in its center. In addition to groceries, she'd also picked up a few things for Stephanie: a cute lamp and a set of brightly colored pillow shams. She pulled the shams out of one of the bags and ran the items upstairs to the spare bedroom. She set the lamp on the nightstand. She ended up making two more trips to the car to retrieve the last of the groceries and the comforter that went with the shams.

She hung her quilted down coat in the laundry room. It was dripping wet. She threw an old towel on the floor beneath it to catch the drops of melting snow.

On her way back to the kitchen, she stopped in front of a long, horizontal mirror. She looked even worse now than when she'd seen herself in the rearview mirror in the parking lot.

Impatiently, she brushed the snowflakes from her hair and pushed a few unruly strands behind her ears. She rubbed at the makeup streaking her face. She'd have to hurry and shower if they were going to make their reservation at Hamiltons. She paused. Could she really sit down for a nice dinner when Carrie was missing? She closed her eyes for a moment. Her outburst at the Providence Center had been much the result of her *own* hard battle, like Brent had said. And, in her heart, she felt Carrie's note wasn't a suicide note.

She prayed she was right.

She'd set the reservation for eight. She'd put things away, shower, and get ready. Then, by the time Paul got home, they could decide what was best to do.

Fishing the smashed bread and rolls from one of the bags, she slapped the packages onto the island. Five of the dozen eggs she'd bought were cracked and had oozed out of their carton, filling the bag with a sticky yellow goo. She should have been more careful putting things into the trunk—what had she been thinking? Somehow, in the next couple of days before Christmas, she'd have to find a few minutes to make yet another trip to the store.

By the time she finished wiping the egg mess from a box of cream cheese and two boxes of snack crackers, the clock on the kitchen wall showed seven fifteen. Placing a package of tortillas in the refrigerator, she bit her lip, wondering if Paul's company plane had been able to land on time. The accumulation of snow was bound to slow things down. It was reasonable to think he might be delayed.

Shoving several canned items into the pantry, the blip of a round light on the answering machine at the end of the breakfast bar caught her eye. For some reason, it made her heart beat faster. Paul was now almost two hours overdue. With everything else going on, it hadn't occurred to her until right then that Paul could possibly have been involved in an accident. She moved toward the phone, hands on her hips, trepidation pulsing through her veins.

In addition to the red light, a numeral three flashed, indicating three new messages. She reached out with one finger and pressed the button, activating the mechanical voice.

"First new message, 2:35 PM. *Hello, Trish? This is Betty Warner. Just wanted to tell you how thankful we are for your efforts to gather food for our shelves here. We really need it. We'll be looking forward to seeing you and the kids tomorrow.*"

Trish dropped her hands to her sides and walked back to the island where she grabbed the rest of the canned goods that belonged in the pantry. The machine droned on.

"Next new message, 4:57 PM. *T.D.?*"

The sound of the voice stopped her cold in her tracks. It was Carrie Hart.

Dropping the cans back onto the island, she rushed toward the answering machine as the message continued.

"*. . . T.D., this is Carrie . . .*"

When Trish first started volunteering at the Providence Center, she and Carrie had gotten off to a bad start. Carrie had accused her of being a "charity hopping snob" who had no real interest in helping troubled kids. The girl had sarcastically coined the moniker "Trish the Dish." As they grew to trust one another, it became something they laughed about—a term of endearment— that Carrie had shortened to T.D.

"*I tried to call you on your cell. I wanted to let you know I wasn't going to be at practice. I'm scared, T.D. I don't know what to do . . .*"

The message ended. Trish replayed it a second time. Carrie's tone was high and rushed. The call had come right before five o'clock, just shortly before Trish got to the Providence Center. She breathed a sigh of relief. At least, as of that time, Carrie seemed to be physically okay. But what had she been afraid of?

Trish's hand shook as she punched in Carrie's number. In her rush, she found she had misdialed, reaching a business downtown. She dialed again. "Please be okay, Carrie. Please answer." Nothing. She hung up the phone and bowed her head as if she were going to pray. Tears rolled down her cheeks, one after another. First slowly, then with more frequency, they fell onto her white blouse. She looked down at them in stunned silence. She wasn't one to cry, but in the past year since Jamie's visit, the act had become increasingly normal to her, a way of letting go of emotion that she once, to her detriment and that of those around her, would have kept bottled inside. Now, as the teardrops fell like a cleansing rain, she decided it felt good.

She didn't know how things would work out, but she knew they would. Carrie had called her. She was thankful for that. Their relationship was intact. She just needed to have faith . . . *faith.*

Right, Jamie?

She plucked a tissue from a box by the phone and dried her tears before gathering up a load of cans from the island and placing them carefully on the shelves of the pantry. As she walked back out into the kitchen, something caught her eye—the manila envelope next to the TV on the counter. She clasped her hands together and blew a breath out through her pursed lips. Her heart thudded in her chest. For some reason, she felt a desperate urgency to hear Paul's voice. She returned to the phone, picked it up, and dialed his cell.

CHAPTER 9

At first, Trish held the phone away from her ear in disbelief. Then she hung up and dialed again.

"At the subscriber's request, this phone number is not currently accepting calls."

It was the same message she'd gotten a second ago. Not accepting calls? What could that mean? She pushed the speed-dial digit three more times in rapid succession, getting the same message each time. Surely there was some sort of mistake. On her fifth try, there was nothing except a short tone like the one that usually followed Paul's invitation for callers to leave a message. There was no message but, after the tone ended, Trish spoke into the phone.

"Paul, honey, where are you?" Her voice broke with a nervous laugh. "Are you okay? I guess you are or I would have heard, right? Anyway, hurry home. Okay? I . . ." She wanted to say something else, sentiment she and Paul hadn't exchanged for longer than she could consciously admit—*I love you.* But she couldn't seem to form the words so she simply said good-bye.

Outside, the giant flakes of snow again began to fall. Trish told herself that was okay—that despite the weather and road conditions, Paul would soon be home, probably in just a matter of minutes. She hadn't realized how much she'd missed him. Not only during his trip but for weeks now, ever since their fight after Sienna left and during all the days she'd kept to herself, not knowing how to make things better.

More tears throbbed at the back of her eyes. She pulled another tissue from the box and, with hesitant steps, approached the envelope. The legal-sized packet bulged with odd shapes at varying intervals. When she touched it, it brought a strange sensation to her fingers, sending a discomforting chill up her spine. The back of the envelope, where the little metal clasp secured the flap—which was taped shut—was blank. Earlier, she'd thought it strange that there was a small white envelope, also blank, taped to the front.

She held the peculiar package with both hands and mulled over where it could have come from and what its contents might be. It hadn't been there yesterday morning; she was sure of it. Right before she'd run errands, she'd placed a few gifts under the tree. When she noticed the envelope, it was on top of those gifts. Had Paul been home without her knowledge? Impossible. He'd been thousands of miles away.

Her intentions were to open the envelope on the breakfast bar where the light was better, but, as she approached, the flashing light on the answering machine once again caught her attention, reminding her there was a third message she'd not yet listened to. She set the envelope down next to the machine and, nervous tension building, alternately rubbed one of her hands and then the other.

A remnant of the aroma of the cookies she'd baked earlier still lingered in the air. She found herself wishing she'd saved one or two for herself. Then she could sit in the roomy breakfast nook at the side of the kitchen on the window seat under the large bay window and have milk and cookies while she watched the snow come down. It would be just like things were "normal"—like in years past when Sienna was little and they'd sat in that very spot together and life hadn't made so many uncomfortable twists and turns.

She sat down on the cushion covering the long bench of the window seat. No milk and cookies; definitely no daughter. Feeling vulnerable and afraid for reasons she couldn't even explain to herself, Trish looked from the answering machine to the envelope then back again to the machine.

When she was little, her father, John, used to bring home treats and hold them behind his back asking, "Which hand?"

Trish and Ann and Robert would respond, "That one," or, "Oh, the other one."

While one of John's hands was empty, the other always contained something wonderful—a few pieces of their favorite candy or a small souvenir he'd picked up somewhere. On special occasions, to their delight, both of his large, calloused hands brought forth wondrous trinkets and goodies.

Trish thought of this childhood game as she looked between her two choices. She had the bottomless, unsettled feeling that neither the answering machine nor the envelope contained good news. An unseen specter seemed to whisper that both, indeed, contained *bad* news. She had no choice—or did she? If she didn't play the message or open the envelope, could she forestall bad news and pain?

After several minutes, she decided she had to do something. She rose to her feet, still wishing for cookies—wait. Hadn't she left a plateful for Paul on the table? Yes. Without a doubt. So many things had happened since she'd left that afternoon, but she definitely *had* left cookies for him. Now the plate was gone. What was going on? She pressed the button on the answering machine.

It was Paul.

"Trish."

He sounded so far away.

"Trish, pick up. Are you there? Did you get the message I left on your cell? I need to talk to you. Call me. I picked up the rest of my things today, but there are details we have to work out. And we need to talk about Sienna. Call me, okay?"

The message ended as unexpectedly as it began, leaving her no clue as to what he meant. Things he picked up? Details to work out? Where was he? He asked if she'd gotten the message he'd left on her cell phone. The phone was still out in the Miata in her purse.

In a daze, she made her way to the front closet to retrieve the pair of boots Paul used when he shoveled snow. Strange—she couldn't seem to locate them. She pushed aside a couple of umbrellas and a backpack. The closet appeared different from what she remembered. There seemed to be other things missing besides the boots. Paul must have moved some things out to the garage.

She found a pair of her old running shoes and pulled them on. She didn't want to make yet another trip to the car in her good shoes, now soaking wet and dripping on the mat by the back door.

The light in the garage illuminated a vast, gaping void where she and Paul, when he was home, usually parked their vehicles side by side. Paul drove a large, sporty Ford pickup, a sharp contrast to her Miata. And on weekends he rode the Harley he'd purchased last fall. She still didn't understand why he'd purchased the motorcycle and why—she quickly did a double take.

It wasn't possible!

She moved toward the far side of the garage. Earlier, when she'd made trips from the car with the groceries, the illumination from the lights outside the garage had been enough to allow her to clearly see her way in and out. Now, however, as she switched on the powerful overhead lights in the garage, it became painfully apparent.

The motorcycle was gone.

How could that be possible? Paul couldn't be driving two vehicles at once!

Despite the cold, beads of perspiration broke out on her forehead. Like an undersea diver awkwardly attempting to return to the surface from whence she'd plunged, Trish fought her way to the garage door and the driveway beyond.

She floundered to the car where she yanked her cell phone from her purse. When she'd put it there—in the parking lot of the grocery store—she must have inadvertently touched something that switched it to silent. She hadn't heard it ring—the chickens— since Lexie first phoned with the news about Carrie.

Not bothering to lock the car, Trish trudged back up the drive while she punched in her voicemail password. Scrolling through new messages from several people, she found the one she was looking for.

The one from Paul.

"Trish, have you seen Sienna? I need you to call me because . . . I can't explain right now but I won't be home tonight. I don't know when I'll be home again or . . . . if."

The phone fell from her grasp. She stared helplessly at the spot in the snow where it landed. The message continued, Paul's voice muffled yet still audible.

"I love you, but there are some things I need to work out. I've gotten most of my stuff out of the house . . . I'm sorry. it has to be this way. I felt I had no choice other than to leave you."

The words hung in the cold night air. She tried to grasp their meaning, but it was out of reach. She struggled to keep herself upright, but a vacuumlike force jerked her downward. It was as if black, foamy water covered her mouth and nose, spilling down her throat and replacing the air in her lungs.

***

How could it be getting warmer? Just seconds ago, it was bitter cold. Or was it a few minutes ago? Or hours? Sienna couldn't tell. Her body stopped shivering, allowing the "warmth" to gradually seep inside of it as she felt herself begin to drift off to sleep.

When the car first left the road, sliding down a short embankment and running up against a tree, she'd frantically searched for her phone. She mentally retraced all the places she'd been. When she'd gone to her mother's house that afternoon to get some decorations for a couple of small Christmas trees she planned to buy, she'd also retrieved a few things from her old room. Her father had called to say he was on his way there, but she'd ended up leaving before he arrived so she could visit Bessie. When she'd finished talking to him, had she left the phone on the nightstand?

Unable to locate it in the car, she pulled on her gloves and struggled out, shoving the door open against the deep, drifted snow with her feet. Assessing the situation while kicking the tires and trying to stamp out flat areas in the frosty white that entombed the car, she quickly realized she was in trouble. Even if she cleared a path so she could move the car away from the tree, she'd never be able to drive the Honda up the embankment.

She'd stomped her way through the deep drifts back up to the road where she stood in the churning snow until she feared she'd freeze to death. She'd heard at least two snowplows drive past before she reached the road, but by the time she got there, not one single car or plow was in sight. Both her Aunt Ann and Uncle Mark and her Uncle Mike lived nearby. She thought she knew the area like the back of her hand. But straining to make out a landmark in the darkness, she couldn't figure out exactly where she was, let alone how close or far away help might be.

Houses along the highway were few and far between, but she could strike out, following what she could tell was the side of the road, and hope to make it to one of them. Was that a safe thing to do, though? What if someone came barreling past and slid into her as she walked? Besides, she had only tennis shoes—and no socks. Her feet wouldn't last long. Better to return to the car and wait out the storm.

Clambering back down the slope and getting into the Honda, she realized just how cold her feet were. She'd turned off the car to save gas. She started it again and tried the heater, punching buttons furiously, to no avail. It only blew cold air. Finally, she shut the engine off, removed her shoes, and sat cross-legged, her feet beneath her for warmth. At one point, they hurt so badly she tried to wrap them in paper napkins from the glove compartment. That didn't work either.

She looked for the phone one more time and began to pray out loud. She'd been praying silently since the car came to rest by the tree. But now, anguished sobs wracked her body, and she began to pray out loud and in earnest. "Please, dear Father in Heaven. Please send my dad. Please help me! I'm so cold."

She'd kept her attention off the stabs of needle-sharp pain in her feet by alternately praying and talking to her Aunt Jamie. As the evening wore on, her determination wore thin.

Now she could only murmur.

Hours ago, her dad must have become worried. He would phone everyone he could think of who might know where she was, even her mother. No one would say they'd seen her. Even if Bessie had a phone, Sienna's father wouldn't contact her—she hadn't told him about the old woman or her plan to visit.

When he couldn't reach her by phone, he would get in his truck and come looking. Had he been in an accident too? Was he somewhere nearby, slowly freezing to death like she was?

She couldn't stand the thought. She loved her father more than she could express. He was all she had. This was her mother's fault—all her mother's fault. If she would have just opened up and shared what it was that always made her so distant and so upset, they could have been a happy family, warm and safe at home and getting ready for Christmas.

But her mother hadn't wanted a family. She'd wanted only material possessions, wanted people to think she was some kind of superwoman. Trish Ingram didn't care one iota for her family. They were dead last on her list. Right?

Sienna swallowed another sob, trying to curb her anger. Grandma Kate had told her what she wanted to know yesterday, and she was slowly beginning to understand just how difficult things had been for her mother all these years. Still, it was no excuse—or was it? Nothing was making sense to her now. Nothing. Especially in the bitter cold that seemed to rob her body of feeling and play tricks on her mind.

Sienna remembered taking a nap once in Grandpa John's boat on Bear Lake. The summer sun had made her drowsy, and the waves on the lake had rocked her back and forth, lulling her to sleep. She felt like she was there now. She could feel waves, the warmth of the sun on her face; she could hear the voices of her family nearby, one in particular. It seemed to be Aunt Jamie . . . but what was she saying? With her last ounce of energy, Sienna strained to hear the words. They came to her like the impression to tap the brakes three times.

Unmistakably, she heard, "Don't go to sleep!"

CHAPTER 10

EVEN MONTHS LATER, WHEN SHE dreamt about Jamie's funeral, Trish could feel the bitter-cold mid-January wind. It lashed at the woolen fabric of her black trench coat and sliced at the exposed skin of her face and hands. As she'd bolted from her car to the mortuary, she'd forgotten her gloves. Her Versace wool scarf had already been hanging around her neck or she likely would have forgotten it as well.

As she'd walked the length of the winding sidewalk, she'd held up one end of the scarf to protect her mouth and chin from the cold. Undeterred by the frigid elements, a somber line of people stood on the steps of the mortuary awaiting their turn to bid farewell to Jamie. Like the keys of a typewriter, the heels of Trish's shoes clicked up the steps. A few people recognized her and stepped aside. Several others, though recognition flashed in their eyes, stood their ground, silently challenging her to go around them.

Whispers spread through the crowd. Trish knew what they were saying: The viewing had started over an hour ago—why wasn't she already inside with the rest of the family?

She brushed aside an ache that seeped into her chest. Why should the opinions of others bother her now? Others had judged Trish her entire life. She didn't need to explain to anyone that although she and Jamie had made their peace, she didn't feel comfortable being with the rest of the family. And, in view of how the "old" Trish had acted for so many years, she felt she didn't deserve the right.

As she squeezed past the mourners to the mortuary doors, she didn't offer them so much as a conciliatory glance, not even what would have been considered an appropriately polite *excuse me*. It wasn't her intention to be rude. If she had to wait like everyone else, she'd lose her nerve. She needed to pay her last respects to Jamie. She had to see this through, no matter whom she offended.

Dozens of floral arrangements spilled into the foyer. The line of people standing outside flowed into the building alongside the flowers, down a short hallway, and into the room that bore Jamie's body. Trish walked past the blur of flowers and the faces of those whose eyes met her with disapproving stares.

The end of the pewter-colored casket was draped with pink roses interspersed with baby's breath. A girl in a white dress held a basket of pink rose petals. Every few seconds, a tear or two would drop from her face and onto the petals. Stephanie. Her black hair pulled back tight against her head in a long ponytail, she looked much older than her eight years.

Stephanie was Jamie's stepdaughter, but the bond they'd shared was as strong as any biological connection. Trish's heart seemed to stop beating for a moment. Though she couldn't remember it at all, Kate McClure had told her of another girl who'd once stood next to a casket containing *her* mother's body in this very same mortuary.

Next to Stephanie stood Mike, who was flanked by Paul and Sienna. Guilt washed over Trish. She should have come earlier, but it had been impossible. She'd had to steel herself for this, taking a few sedatives her doctor prescribed and mentally coaching herself, over and over, on exactly what she needed to do.

The looks she got as she walked up to the casket were severe. Out of the corner of her eye, she saw Paul's head drop. Cutting in front of another mourner, she laid her left hand on the side of the casket and forced herself to look down.

Jamie was dressed in white. At her request, a small bouquet of wild flowers had been placed in her hands. She looked so peaceful yet so very, very still. Trish began to quaver as the old, familiar feeling of rushing, black water sucked at her feet.

She steadied herself and put her hand into her coat pocket, gently extracting a gold chain from its depths. The chain had once been part of a necklace that bore two halves of a gold heart. Now, only one half remained. The other was gone forever.

Just above Jamie's hands and to the side of the flowers, Trish laid the chain. She brought the fingers of her left hand to her lips then moved them away a few inches, blowing a good-bye kiss. "Thank you," she whispered. Even then, though she felt tears at the corners of her eyes, she didn't allow herself to weep.

When she stepped back, her feet became entangled in her scarf, which somehow had become so lopsided on her neck that one end now hung to the floor. She stumbled and fell, rolling onto her back. Kate and Ann rushed to her side. A moment later, Paul and Sienna were there as well. Feeling stupid and embarrassed, Trish waved them all away and clambered to her feet by herself.

Sienna backed away, shaking her head. Involuntarily, Trish's hand shot toward her daughter, trying to reach out to the child she loved so much. But Sienna only moved farther away.

In that moment, Trish would have given anything, even her life, to make Sienna understand that both her unconventional entrance into the mortuary and her refusal of help were because of her own demons, not because she was the brazen, heartless being everyone assumed she was. But Sienna didn't understand, and the look on her face sent a sharp dagger of pain into Trish's heart.

The dream was the same every night, and it was at this point, with Trish feeling the full force of Sienna's wrath, that it usually stopped. Then, afterward, there was always an accompanying period of semiconscious review wherein Trish's brain would replay her options—what she could have or should have done differently.

She could have waited in line like the rest of the mourners, not giving the impression she thought of herself above them. Or she could have not gone to the funeral at all, but that was out of the question. She owed a debt to Jamie. She should have accepted Paul's invitation to go to the mortuary early with him and Sienna, but she simply hadn't felt worthy enough to do that.

Tonight, however, there was no "period of review."

The dream continued to another phase, one Trish didn't remember having before. This time, after getting to her feet, she walked out of the viewing room and was just about to exit the building when she noticed a small room off to her right with yet another casket.

There were no people in this room, and, unlike Jamie's, this casket was unadorned—no flowers were draped over its shiny black exterior. In fact, there were no flowers anywhere in the room. Trish's steps became stiff and calculated. She walked toward the casket and grasped its side with both hands to steady herself. Like sand filling up an empty hourglass, terror started at her feet then rose quickly, filling her legs and torso, then her arms and neck. When it reached her chin, her mouth opened and she started to scream.

The casket was full of black, foamy water.

The sight jarred Trish into full consciousness. She sat bolt upright in her own bed, pulling her breaths out of the thick, molasses-like silence that filled the house. She looked around. There was no water. It was a dream.

Only a dream.

Between breaths, she found herself straining to hear any sound that might signal a human presence—hopefully Paul or Sienna—any indication that someone cared enough to come home and find out if she was all right.

A sob broke from her throat. It had been her choice not to tell Paul when they got married that she wasn't really a McClure—her choice not to tell him that she'd never had a father; her choice to not tell and instead try to forget that her unmarried mother had committed suicide right in front of her. She'd wanted to protect Paul, and later, Sienna, but her life of lies had been the undoing of her family.

For a moment, she thought about lying back down and trying to return to sleep, maybe even an endless sleep . . . The sedatives she'd gotten after Jamie's death were in the medicine cabinet. She could easily imagine herself sleeping into eternity in her four poster mahogany bed. Would anyone come to see what had happened to her when she didn't arrive at the nursing home or at the Providence Center? Would the Christmas program at the tabernacle just go on without her, perhaps in spite of her, like she never existed? After the way she'd acted last night in front of Lexie and the kids, she wouldn't blame anyone for wanting to forget her.

She rubbed her hands roughly over her face. No, no one would come. At least not until the bank came to repossess the house.

That thought was enough to propel her to the edge of the bed. She would push on, no matter what. She would force the elements in her life, now so staggeringly out of balance, back into her control.

Suicide was not an option.

Like someone taping a torn photograph back together, bits and pieces of what happened the night before began to come together in her head.

They didn't make a pretty picture.

Her soggy clothes lay in a pile between the end of the bed and the archway that led to the double vanity and bathroom beyond. Last night, after hearing Paul's message and falling into the snow, she'd forced herself to move up the driveway to the house. She'd thought, at first, that someone had pulled her up out of the snow, but there hadn't been anyone in sight. In fact, if any of the neighbors had seen her, they'd given no indication.

What kind of a neighborhood did she live in where people ignored a woman crawling through the snow without at least checking to see if she was okay?

Maybe they didn't dare. How many of them, after all, had been at Jamie's funeral and witnessed that she wouldn't even accept the help of her own family?

She'd changed, hadn't she? Why couldn't everyone see that? Why couldn't Sienna see it? Why couldn't Paul? It didn't matter. She could only blame herself.

Trish picked up a hairbrush, intending to untangle some of the knots from her disheveled hair. Instead, she threw it at her reflection in the long mirror that stretched the length of the vanity. Oh, how she hated that reflection now!

She'd tried to remake herself. Why had her relationships with others been completely destroyed? It had been when she'd given up control and tried to turn her life around and trust in the power of the gift Jamie had given her—in the power of love—that things had begun to spiral downward. Maybe she hadn't really changed. It seemed her efforts hadn't made any difference. At least the "old" Trish still had her family at home a year ago.

She stormed into the shower. Turning on the water as hot as she could stand it, she scrubbed until her skin was raw. She was determined to emerge from the water strong and in charge of her destiny.

After doing her hair and makeup, she yanked a black cardigan and dyed-to-match silk blouse from their hangers. She looked again at the pile of damp clothing near the bathroom. After she had gone back into the house last night, she'd lain on the floor just inside the door by the garage for a long time. It was sometime after one o'clock in the morning when she'd made it up the stairs and finally cast off her wet clothing before dragging herself into bed.

A persistent, piercing coldness had been her companion throughout the night. The shower hadn't diminished it. It was more than just physical. It reminded her there were things in the past she didn't want to face. She shoved it aside. She had things to do.

She put on designer jeans and sat on her side of the bed to tug on a pair of black boots. What was she saying? Her side of the bed? Now both sides of the bed were hers.

She picked up the phone from its cradle on the nightstand. It felt as cold and hard in her hand as her heart felt in her chest.

CHAPTER 11

"Pick up, Ann. Pick up! Where are you?" Trish studied the dust on the tall bedposts. A series of cobwebs ran from one post and over to the wall. The carpet needed to be vacuumed. She should never have let Etta, her part-time housekeeper, go last spring. She'd thought she could do all the housework on her own—Mrs. Domesticity herself. Well, a fine job she'd done.

The house, like her life, was going to pieces.

The phone continued to ring. Her sister Ann didn't believe in owning an answering machine, always claiming that someone with anything important to say would call back. Well, Trish had something important to say, and if she had to let the phone ring for the rest of that Tuesday morning or for the rest of the day, she was going to say it!

On what Trish counted as the eighth ring, Ann finally answered.

"Hello?" Ann's voice sounded tired. "Hello . . ."

Trish pushed a few strands of hair behind her ears. "You weren't still in bed, were you?" Trish asked, trying to sound composed. "It's past seven, isn't it? I thought you farm types were up and going with the chickens." She'd intended the comment to contain some degree of levity, but in her present state of mind, the words grated.

"Trish," Ann gasped. "Have you seen Sienna?"

"No . . . I haven't . . . I was calling . . ."

"Trish," Ann tried to interrupt.

Thinking only of her inner turmoil, Trish forced out her words while she still had the stamina to do so. "Ann, remember that lawyer you and Mark hired a couple of years ago?" she asked. "The

one who settled the property-line dispute for you? I need his name.
Do you think he handles divorce?"

The line was silent. Then Ann spoke slowly, her tone guarded.
"Who needs a lawyer, Trish?"

"I do." There was another long pause on the end of the line.
Trish switched the phone to her other ear and pressed her fingers
to her forehead.

"You want to explain?" asked Ann.

"No, not really."

"Trish, who is getting divorced?"

"Paul and I, or should I say Paul? I'm just going to cut to the
chase and do it for him." .

"Oh, Trish. I thought you were over all this."

"What's that supposed to mean?"

"I thought you'd worked through some of your issues. I
thought I'd seen a change in you . . ."

Trish bristled. "I've made changes, Ann. I've made up for past
mistakes; I've come a long way. It's Paul who's stayed where he
was."

"Is that so bad?"

"Ann, you know what I'm talking about. I'm a good person . . .
I . . ."

"Whether you're a good person has never been in question."

"Well, it must be, or you wouldn't have made that remark. *I
thought you were over all this!*"

"Okay, okay. Back up. Maybe that was out of line, but let me
ask just one question. All these 'changes' in your life—did you
bother to explain them to Paul?"

Trish recoiled. "I can see where this is going, Ann. You're on
Paul's side. You never saw my side of things."

"On the contrary—I think I saw them very well." Ann paused
and cleared her throat. "That's why I was so excited when you told
me about Jamie, about her gift and what it meant to you. But you
didn't answer my question. Did you tell Paul about Jamie's visit?
Did you tell him why you were doing what you were doing? Did
you try giving the gift to Paul and Sienna, or just to the elderly and
the kids at the Providence Center?"

"Let's not drag my volunteer work into this. I'm through with all that anyway. Everything I've done . . . well, it hasn't mattered a hill of beans, has it? Look where it's gotten me."

"Oh, Trish, I really wish you'd explain what's going on."

"What's going on? I'll tell you." The phone in her right hand, her left hand waved as she spoke. "Paul has left me. When he bought that motorcycle I knew we were headed for trouble. I wouldn't be surprised if he's riding around with a cute young redhead on the back right now!"

"Oh, Trish. Listen to yourself. Paul having an affair? You know he'd never—"

"I know nothing of the sort. Who can blame him? Married so long to someone like me—he was ready for a change."

"Trish, honestly. Get a grip, will you?"

"I headed to your house last night to talk to you about something else—I needed someone to talk to," Trish mumbled. "But I knew you wouldn't understand; you never have."

"Understand what, Trish? Talk to me now."

"Let's just say screwing up is in my genes—look at my mother and my father, whoever he may be."

"Trish. Stop feeling so sorry for yourself."

"How dare you, Ann." Jumping up from the bed, Trish hissed, "You McClures and your pompous attitudes. You have no idea what it's like to be on the other side, to try to live in a perfect world when you're imperfect and to find, no matter what you do, that no one recognizes you as equal."

"Is that why you've done everything you've done, Trish? Because you thought it would earn you some kind of recognition? In your words, make you equal?" Ann went on. "Remember that windmill puzzle Grandma McClure had in her front closet, and how we worked on it all day only to discover some pieces missing?"

"What does that have to do with anything?"

"You nearly tore the closet apart looking for them. You never did find them, and you cried all the way home. After that, you never wanted to put another puzzle together. You said 'What's the use? Go to all that work only to find out you don't have all the pieces.'"

Trish remembered now—the feelings of frustration and uselessness.

"Well, Trish, that's the way your life is. You think you don't have everything you were supposed to have, so you dwell on the lost pieces and neglect to see the beauty in the pieces you do have."

Trish jumped in. "You didn't have to find out by looking at a photo album that you weren't even part of the family you thought was yours."

"For better or worse, Trish, you *are* a McClure. I've heard all this a hundred times before—all our lives. I don't want to hear it anymore. I'm tired of it. I have problems too. They may not be like yours, but I am not immune to pain, and I am not perfect—no one in this family ever said or pretended they were but you, dear sister."

Trish laughed. "I'm not your sister."

"Then I guess you shouldn't be calling me."

Trish heard Ann slam the receiver into the cradle on her end then the buzz of the dial tone.

So much for regaining control of her life.

***

IF HE'D SLEPT AT ALL, Paul didn't remember.

All night long, he'd tossed and turned on the couch in Sienna's living room. Yesterday afternoon, she'd said she was going to visit someone, but for how long? By the time the clock struck half past eight last night, he was worried—really worried. He'd tried and tried to reach Sienna on her cell, but it went straight to voice mail. He began calling everyone he could think of, even Trish. But there was no answer at the house, and her cell went straight to voice mail as well. Ann hadn't seen Sienna. Mike hadn't seen her either, but he had mentioned something strange. Trish had visited him yesterday, they'd had a good visit, and he was in agreement with everything.

What was up with that? Paul thought Trish hated Mike.

He'd been so worried about Sienna he told Mike he'd talk to him about whatever it was later.

By the time nine o'clock rolled around, he was frantic. There had still been no answer at the house, so he called the highway patrol, asking about accidents. None involving a red Accord or a nineteen-year-old girl had been reported. When the highway patrol

called him back, saying the snow plows had done a cursory sweep
of Highway 89 around ten PM, they said there wasn't a car in sight.

Where was his daughter?

He'd called all Sienna's friends, but they said the same thing:
they hadn't seen her. A couple of them said she'd probably stayed
with this or that friend until the storm was over. But every friend
Paul called said they hadn't seen her either. Sienna would have
called if she'd intended to be gone all night, wouldn't she? But
then again, she'd been on her own for over six months now—she
probably wasn't used to checking in anymore.

Still, Paul couldn't shake the feeling that something was wrong.

He grabbed the phone from where he'd put it under his pillow.
His feet hitting the floor, he punched in the number to the house.
Busy. So Trish was home now. Or was she? If someone else was
calling at the same time— or leaving a message—there would
be a busy signal just as though someone were using the line. He
punched in the number for Trish's cell. No answer. Only her
message. *"This is Trish Ingram. I'm away from the phone right now.
Please call again."*

Paul felt like cursing, but he held his tongue.

Since he'd slept in his clothes, all he had to do was pull on
his black leather jacket. He headed out to his truck but, taking in
the now-cleared roads and the glimmering of a bright December
sunrise, he changed his mind and mounted the Harley.

He was going to find his daughter. And his wife.

CHAPTER 12

December 7, 1967

D<small>EAR</small> C<small>ECILE</small>,
I got your letter. Thanks! And thanks for keeping me up to date on everything at home. I can't believe "The Dick Van Dyke Show" isn't going to be on TV anymore. What about the other good stuff, like "Get Smart" and "Batman"?

Thanks, too, for keeping me up to date on Willie Mays—you know I think he's the greatest ballplayer ever. One of the guys here has a poster of Mays he says I can have when our outfit goes home next spring—don't get too excited yet. I don't have a date; it could even be next summer or into fall. I'll let you know.

Did you hear about Muhammad Ali? I guess it happened a while ago, news is so slow getting here, but he refused to fight. Some of the guys think it's not fair if he doesn't have to. As for me, I try not to judge men for what they believe in. Some people think we're crazy to be here. Remember all those protests we saw on TV? I don't agree with everything, I don't like doing what I'm doing most of the time, but I'm proud to be representing my country. It's important to me.

Take good care of yourself and write when you can. If you need anything, please ask my uncle or my mother. They'll help you.

Much love,

Your Snack Bar Guy

CHAPTER 13

December 21, 2010

OVERWHELMED WITH PAIN AND ANGUISH, Trish flew down the stairs to the family room. If she had to spend Christmas alone, she'd do it on her own terms. She'd take down every last Christmas decoration, removing any and all vestiges of the holiday, then clean the house from top to bottom. She didn't need Etta. She didn't anyone. The thought gave her strength. She could control her destiny. She could do things on her own, in a way that pleased her. No one else mattered.

Why did she think she needed Ann's help? She'd find a divorce lawyer on her own. As part of the settlement, she'd sell the house and go away—far away—and start over. Not moving far away from Utah when she and Paul were first married had been a major mistake. She'd thought the mere forty miles she'd put between herself and where she'd grown up would be enough—she'd been dead wrong. Now she would remedy that and forge herself into the type of woman she admired, a strong woman—like her Women of the Attic. She'd build herself back up. If anyone ever spoke of her again it would be to say, "Look at Trish Ingram—she's as tough as nails. Nothing can get her down. She's doing it all on her own."

Using the words to cement together the scarred and broken pieces of her heart, she built a mental wall, thick and high.

She lashed into the tree, tearing decorations off and throwing them onto the floor. She felt a sharp stab of pain in the end of her left forefinger. The cut was long and deep, but she ignored it like she ignored the sounds of the breaking ornaments. She reached as high as she could without getting the ladder out of the garage, then abandoned the tree and whisked around the room, ripping down the inside wreaths from each of the four doors that led from the family room onto the wraparound cement patio.

She moved to the burgundy candles sitting on top of the piano and end tables, and then to the ivy and pine centerpieces on the sofa tables, grabbing everything and throwing it into one big pile in the middle of the family room. Maybe she could just shove everything into the fireplace and light a match. That would be a fitting end to the "season of joy," wouldn't it?

Pausing for a moment, she noticed something wet—blood. Her finger oozed a steady stream of bright red. Droplets were spattered here and there on the carpet and her clothing. She rushed to the kitchen sink, cupping the finger in her right hand. Cold water streamed from the faucet as she yanked the handle into its on position. She scrubbed the blood off both her hands and inspected the finger. The bleeding showed no signs of stopping. She wrapped a paper towel around the wound and stormed to the entryway.

Tugging a pine swag off the wall, Trish looked down at the hall table, where Sienna's handmade nativity was laid out, and felt an electric-like force pass through her body. The plastic baby Jesus slept peacefully in his manger. She threw the swag onto the tiled floor and picked the baby up. Tears blazed behind her eyes, but she stifled them.

She cupped the baby Jesus in both hands and walked down the hall toward the kitchen. "Why?" she beseeched the plastic figurine. "Why can't I ever make things right?"

Her emotions boiling like lava inside a volcano, Trish felt as though she were going to explode. The tiny baby Jesus in her hands seemed to evoke the only saving peace that kept her from spontaneous combustion.

Shaking and out of breath, she dropped to her knees next to the window seat in the breakfast nook and put the baby Jesus into the pocket of her sweater. She bowed her head and closed her eyes. "Please . . . please . . . please!" were the only words she could manage to utter as she rocked her body forward and back. Hands clasped together on her lap, she noticed the feeling of wetness again. She opened her eyes and saw that the paper towel was soaked through with blood.

Trish stood up and walked to the sink to get another paper towel. The winter storm that had wrapped the area in white was over. Rays of morning sunlight shone through the big bay window into the kitchen, illuminating a space on the breakfast bar. Her eyes followed the rays, and she saw something she'd forgotten—the manila envelope that still sat next to the answering machine.

After rewrapping her finger, Trish reached out. Touching the parcel once again made the hair on the back of her neck stand on end. Why did the envelope have that effect? Fighting a wave of dizziness, she leaned against the bar for support. She pulled the smaller envelope off the larger one and opened it. There was a note inside.

The handwriting was Sienna's.

"Mom, thought you might need these things. Love, Sienna."

"Sienna!" Trish gasped, clutching the note to her chest. "Oh, Sienna." Her thoughts flashed like wildfire to her family. She hadn't meant to drive them away. She didn't really want to be alone. She didn't really want to go back to the empty existence that marked the life of the "old" Trish.

Body and soul aching, Trish used a butter knife to cut open the tape sealing the large envelope. She bent the clasp back and let the contents slide out onto the gray marble countertop.

Where on earth had Sienna gotten these things and how? Why did she think Trish needed them? Her heart pounding, Trish gently ran her fingertips over the items: a lock of auburn hair with a bright blue ribbon tied around it, two black-and-white photos of a woman with straight hair holding a baby, and a third photo she recognized of herself as a child.

There was also a photo of a headstone.

She quickly turned her attention away from that and picked up an old pocket watch.

Engraved with the initials R. C., it was fastened to a short length of thin gold chain. Prying open the clasp with her fingernails, Trish found that the face of the watch had been smashed as if someone had deliberately hit it with a blunt object. The hands were forever stopped at 11:35.

Nausea boiled in Trish's stomach. She fought it off and put the watch down.

Two additional objects remained—a folded piece of yellowed paper and something heavy wrapped inside layers of tattered, rose-colored fabric. Trish picked up the fabric packet. Inside she found a rock. A little smaller than a piece of bread, the inch-thick rock had been skillfully painted to resemble a resting swan with its head tucked against its wing. Its black eye looked sharp and wise, its feathers a beautiful white shaded with strokes of cream.

Trish turned the swan over. The tiny brushstrokes that formed the feathers wrapped around the sides of the rock but stopped when they reached the back. In the middle of the back was a white heart bearing pink paintbrush strokes that formed the initials C. A.

The swan seemed to grow uncomfortably warm in Trish's hands. She set it down and picked up the piece of yellowed paper and unfolded it. Hands shaking, she began to read.

My dearest Trisha Amelia . . . They say suicide is a selfish act, one that at least temporarily absolves the person who commits it from their cares but one that leaves those left behind with a legacy of pain . . .

If Trish's heart continued beating, she wasn't aware of it. A black tide of angry water surged in her throat. Fighting overwhelming emotion, she carefully but quickly shoved all the contents back into the envelope and struggled to push herself away from the bar and stand upright. She desperately needed to flee to a secure place where she could read the rest of the letter.

***

"I'M GLAD YOU DECIDED TO come home for Thanksgiving." Her mother's words soothed Sienna as they sat together on the window seat in the breakfast nook.

"Me too, Mom. The turkey smells so good."

"Thanks." Trish looked over at the timer on the oven. *"It ought to be done in an hour. So tell me how your classes are going."*

"Great. I mean, overall. They're tough, but I'm really enjoying them—as much as you can enjoy finance and business. Did Dad tell you they might have a spot for me next year at E-Quip?"

Her mother looked out the window. "I think he did mention it . . . you know we haven't had much time to talk lately."

"Make time, Mom." She saw the startled look in her mother's eyes and, like in countless times past, she thought she'd pushed too hard. The hard edge to her mother's voice had softened since the passing of her Aunt Jamie, though, and now she only put her hand on Sienna's.

"Yes, I need to. You know I love your father, don't you?"

"Of course, Mom. Why would you even ask such a thing?"

"Because I haven't always been good at showing him, or you."

"But you're doing better. I'm proud of you."

"You really think so?"

"Yes." Sienna took a drink of apple cider. The conversation seemed to be going so well she thought she'd delve a little deeper. "How come you never told Dad that you volunteer at the Providence Center? How come you never told me?"

"I don't know . . . Over the years, Dad and I have both fallen into a pattern of doing things our own way. Your dad has his work—you know how much he travels. And his riding friends. I've always had something else going too—shopping, my Bunko group, attending decorating classes, giving parties for everyone at your dad's work . . ."

"Or for everyone in the Chamber of Commerce, or the neighborhood, or the Ladies League . . ." Sienna took a bite of the pumpkin bread her mother had made and another sip of cider. "That still doesn't answer my question. You haven't done any of that for a long time now but, yesterday, you said you've been at the center since February."

Her mother cut her another piece of pumpkin bread. "You were surprised when you saw me there, weren't you?"

Sienna chewed and said around half a mouthful, "Yeah, a little. Well, okay, a lot."

Her mother nodded. "I'm glad you came by. You can't imagine how good it was for me to see you. Every time I call, you're always so busy . . . I mean, I know that's my fault. I've never really fostered a close relationship with you."

"Mom, we're both working on that now. And I'm carrying a full class load. It really is hard for me to break free. I stopped by the center because I missed Aunt Jamie and because I wanted to see if there was anything I could do for the kids and their families. But I was on my way here. Really. But . . ."

"But I still haven't answered your question, have I? I never told your dad I was volunteering there because there were lots of emotional strings attached that I simply didn't know how to explain. I'm trying to get to it, really. Sienna, it's hard to explain, but I feel I have to prove myself."

"Prove yourself. What do you mean?"

"I'll try to explain. My sixth-grade teacher's name was Mrs. Taylor. She was a nice grandma-type lady—I really loved her. When the end of the year was coming, I wanted to make her something special. I knew she liked roses so I decided to draw one of the most beautiful roses I could; I worked and worked. Sometimes I got discouraged and threw away what I was working on and started over. I went through about a half-dozen pink, red, and green colored pencils. Finally, with only a few days left until the end of the school year, I got it right. I gave her that rose and—the look in her eyes—I could tell she was so proud of me. That's the way it is with your dad, Sienna. I want him to be proud of me as well. I've worked hard on being a better person and getting everything in my life sorted out. I want to make sure I've done my best . . . before I feel I can deserve to have a good relationship with him. Before I feel worthy of it."

"You know what? Did you ever think that Mrs. Taylor might have loved you just the same after you gave her the rose as before? Mom, Dad loves you right now. You don't have to prove anything to him."

"Oh, but, sweetie, I do. It's complicated. There are lots of things you don't know, things I've tried to protect both you and Dad from for a long time. Jamie helped me see I was headed down the wrong path. I realized I needed—wanted—to do things differently. She asked if I was happy, Sienna. I knew I was far from it, and I didn't think I deserved to be—I didn't think someone like me deserved to be happy."

"Mom, I've seen you nearly kill yourself trying to prove something to others—I never knew what. You're a beautiful woman, a beautiful person, gifted in every way but . . . it never seems good enough." Sienna shifted in the window seat and sat cross-legged. *"We talked about this after Aunt Jamie died. I told you I always thought it was Dad and I who weren't good enough for you. You told me then that wasn't it—but that's all you said. Mom, I know there's something from your past that troubles you. Please tell me about it. Please let me help."*

"Sienna, some things are better left unsaid."

"I'm sorry. I don't agree. Remember when I was in the sixth grade—that mean substitute we had, Mrs. Rawlinson? She always made fun of us when we got problems wrong in math. When you found out, you wondered why I never told you. You said I should always talk to you and that you would help me because you're my mom." Sienna fingered the edge of her cider cup. *"And you were right—most of the time. I could talk to you about anything—anything except about you or about our family. If I did,"* Sienna drank the rest of her cider and braced herself, *"you would shut me out."*

She watched as her mother turned away. *"You don't need to handle my problems, Sienna. I'm the grown-up. I need to do it on my own. I might not have handled things as best as I could—believe me, if I had it all to do over again, I'd do things quite differently—but it's too late to go back now."*

"It's never too late." Sienna put her hand on her mother's knee.

Her mother didn't say anything. Instead, she picked up her cup, and Sienna's, and began to clear the table.

"Can I say one more thing, Mom?"

"What, sweetie?"

"I know last year you thought Jamie just left Uncle Mike and Stephanie and ran off somewhere."

"Sienna, whatever I thought is water under the bridge. I may not have understood everything your aunt did, but I have great respect for her. I made judgments I shouldn't have. I was wrong. For whatever else she did in her life, Jamie was a very loving person. Anyone just has to look at what she started at the Providence Center to see that."

"True, but there's something you need to know."

Her mother put the cider cups into the sink and turned on the water. *"I forgive her, Sienna. Whatever her reasoning, I forgive her. I owe her a great debt."*

"Mom, Aunt Jamie went to Omaha to see Grandma Kate."

The water shut off. Now it was Sienna who stared out the window, too afraid to meet her mother's gaze. *"She asked Grandma Kate what it was about your childhood that made you so upset."*

"She what?"

"She loved you, Mom. Before she died she wanted to help in any way she could. She and I both had known for a long time that something bad happened to you."

"She went to talk to Grandma Kate?" The tone in her mother's voice was strained and raspy. "What right did she have to do that? What did Grandma . . . tell her?"

Sienna shut her eyes like when she was little and she knew her mother was mad. "I don't know, Mom. Jamie wouldn't say. She just said it had something to do with December 20. That's why she went to see you on that day last year. She said it was a hard day for you and she wanted you to know that she loved you."

"What else did she say, Sienna? Who else did she tell?"

"Don't get angry, okay? She was trying to help."

"Help? By sticking her nose into my business? Then dragging you into it?"

"She didn't drag me into anything." Sienna stood and stalked to the counter, now facing her mother. "I wanted her to talk to Grandma Kate. I was tired of all the lies and all the secrets. Tired of being kept in the dark while you pretended I wasn't even alive."

"I never did that. You know I did my best by you."

"What I know is that there was—and still is—a part of you that you never gave to me and Daddy. A part that you keep hidden that makes you angry and afraid."

"That is my business, Sienna. My business! Not yours and Jamie's."

Not yours and Jamie's . . .

"Mama!" Sienna cried out. She flailed against the steering wheel in the car. *The steering wheel.* She'd been dreaming about the fight she and her mother had at Thanksgiving, but she was so cold and so tired that it had seemed real. "Mama," she cried again.

The fight had been terrible. When her father had walked in, both she and her mother were shouting. Sienna had threatened to leave the house and never return. Her mother told her it was probably just as well. Neither of them would tell her father what they'd been arguing about or why.

Days later, her father said he and her mother had argued as well, after she left. Sienna was torn apart. If she told her father the whole thing about Jamie and Grandma Kate, her mother would never forgive her. She was caught in a web of lies that was not of her own making. The only thing she could do was retreat further away. During the first week in December, she realized that retreating wasn't a solution when she found herself feeling so despondent she could barely leave her apartment. She dropped two classes—she couldn't deal with the stress. She was more convinced than ever that something bad had happened to her mother.

She had to know the truth.

She wrote to her grandmother and poured out her heart. In response, Grandma Kate had called—Sunday morning—and Sienna had finally gotten the answers she was looking for. At least part of them.

"Mama, I'm sorry. I didn't mean to make you angry. I can see now why you were hurt." She reached out. Was her mother really there, or was she just imagining it?

She reached over onto the passenger seat and found the second to the last of the cookies—the cookies she'd taken from the table at the house. She took a couple of small bites and forced herself to chew. She knew she had to keep up her strength, but she was tired—so very tired. Her fingers clumsy and nearly unresponsive, she reached for the last cookie, wrapped it in a paper napkin, and put it into her pocket.

From somewhere came a sound—maybe part of the dream. Barking. A dog. With her last bit of strength, Sienna tried to rub a clear spot on the driver's side window. But the condensation from her breath was frozen solid on the glass.

She couldn't see a thing.

CHAPTER 14

ENVELOPE IN HAND, HER BODY tense, Trish made her way to the attic staircase. She flipped the light on and ascended, holding tight to the narrow railing. In the attic, she walked across the dusty expanse of floor over what was Sienna's room and then the guest room. There, the attic took a jog out over the master bedroom. Clutching the envelope with both hands now, Trish slowed her steps.

Immediately in front of her, a massive brick chimney rose through the floor, continuing up through the roof several feet above her head. A dozen or so large boxes were piled high to one side of it. Trish had arranged them herself, cramming in as many in as possible to give the illusion that the area at the side of the chimney was full and impassable. Stepping close to the chimney, she squeezed between it and a couple of tall boxes that held old clothing. After a few steps, the area beside the chimney opened. There, tucked next to the slanting roofline and the bricks was her old pine dresser—the one she'd used growing up in the McClure household.

Faded from the years, the once bright yellow dresser was about five feet long. Underneath the vanity was a small bench. Trish pulled out the bench and sat down. This was her private place; the only place she felt safe, away from the prying eyes and minds of the world.

The vanity's desk was topped by an inlaid, horizontal mirror. At the back of the dresser, another mirror, large and round, stretched up, almost touching the timbers of the attic roofline. Around this mirror were taped photos of all different shapes and sizes. These were Trish's Women of the Attic.

She hadn't always referred to them that way. As a teenager, when she became obsessed with making herself into a strong, successful woman who bore no traces of the ashes she'd risen from, she began to collect the photographs so she'd have models to pattern her life after. It was only after she and Paul moved here and she found herself still needing what they represented that she'd put them back on the mirror and coined the term.

She let her eyes trail the familiar photos. Politicians and musicians, authors and actresses, two noteworthy doctors and a professor—they had all fit Trish's ideal of strong women, either in looks or in manner or both.

In the middle of the mirror, where Trish's face should have appeared, was a collage of photos. Some from area newspapers and a few from old yearbooks, they were all of a blond woman with severe eyebrows and a firm yet attractive smile—Lynette Campion. Undeniably the most beautiful, popular, and wealthy woman in the county where Trish grew up, Lynette had been everything Trish always wanted to be.

Trish put the envelope on the mirrored vanity top. The paper towel on her finger was beginning to soak through again. Though the bleeding had slowed considerably, she replaced the paper towel with a few Kleenexes from a box on the dresser. Aware that her breathing was sharp and rapid, she consciously forced herself to slow it, and, after a few moments' hesitation, she reached into the envelope for the letter.

She unfolded it and began to read again.

***

PANIC FILLED PAUL INGRAM. IT was nearly eleven AM Tuesday morning, and he still had not been unable to locate Sienna.

He gunned his motorcycle up and down the length of Interstate 15, from Ogden to Brigham City and back to the first Ogden exit on the south. On his cell phone, he again called the highway patrol. Their answer was the same as last night: no car matching the description he'd given them of Sienna's red Honda had been seen on the side of any road in either Box Elder or Weber counties.

Overhead, the sun shone brightly. The interstate itself was dry, but the nearly foot-and-a-half-high snow drifts in the median and on the sides of the north and southbound lanes were evidence of the savage winter storm that had passed through the area last night.

Paul swung off the interstate onto the 1100 South exit, heading east into town. Here, the road was still slushy in spots. East of the intersection where 1100 South met Brigham City's Main Street, Paul stopped on the side of the canyon road that led to Logan. Mike had already scanned the sides of the old highway—Highway 89—and the edges of the orchards from Brigham to Ogden three times and was now checking the side roads. The highway patrol said their officers had been over the canyon nearly a half-dozen times that morning, but Paul wanted to recheck it and get to the house, where there was still no answer when he called.

Before heading home, he made one more call on his cell phone. He needed all the help he could get.

CHAPTER 15

*M*Y DEAREST *TRISHA AMELIA* . . . *THEY say suicide is a selfish act,
one that at least temporarily absolves the person who commits it
from their cares but one that leaves those left behind with a legacy of
pain . . .*

Trish's fingers tensed, wrinkling the edges of the paper. She
read on.

*Your Aunt Kate loves you, Trish. Many a time she has cared for
you when I was mentally unable. Those times seem to be coming more
and more frequently and, as much as I always want to be near you, I
fear in my diminished state that I will not be able to attend to all your
needs.*

*One day, I pray you will be able to understand that if it had
not been for the lives I was responsible for ending and the mockery I
have inadvertently made of all who loved me, ruining their lives and
reputations, I would never consider this act.*

*That it is selfish is true, but I know no other way. No one
understands the burdens that crush me. Should I stay on this earth, I
fear they would crush you too . . ."*

There were more words, but Trish had had enough. Who had
Sienna gotten the letter from? Kate? Whoever it was had betrayed
Trish—betrayed her by revealing the secrets of her past to her
daughter. Obviously, Sienna, knowing the truth, had told Paul.
Now Trish could comprehend his disdain for her—she was a fraud.

Trish's fingers tensed at the edges of the paper, creasing it
deeply. A dark smear of blood seeped onto the right-hand side.
Her finger was bleeding again. Mechanically, she began to crumple
the paper into a wad. She could see no reason, no need, no good in
reading the letter now, especially after all these years.

One day, I pray you will be able to understand . . .

If Trish lived to be a hundred, she would never understand. There was no excuse—none. What kind of mother could write something like this, trying to explain herself as though she loved and cared for her child, but then force that child out into a cold, dark night to be the unwitting witness of . . .

. . . the lives I was responsible for ending . . .

Why had she written that? The only lives this woman ended were her own and Trish's.

Bile formed in Trish's mouth, the black water again seeming to rise in her throat. Bright pinpricks of white light filled her vision. She felt as though she were going to lose consciousness. She didn't care. She was tired of fighting for her sanity, tired of pretending, tired of life. It would be so simple for Paul and Sienna if she just packed her things and went away for good.

Downstairs, she could hear the faint but persistent ringing of the house phone. Maybe Ann calling back. Maybe—but likely not—Paul. She'd heard it earlier and ignored it.

It didn't matter.

The photos on the mirror in front of her dimmed and blurred. She let herself sink deeper into the water of her nightmares; she didn't struggle. It rose to her chin, her mouth . . .

A thump on the other side of the boxes sliced into Trish's senses and startled her from her thoughts. She stood abruptly.

"Who's there? Paul? Sienna? Answer me."

Her legs wobbly, she sank back onto the bench. It seemed she was still alone, and yet . . .The ringing of the phone was much louder now. It seemed so close, as though it was on the other side of the boxes.

Trish rose to her feet again, this time gradually, and forced herself to take a few tentative steps away from the dresser. "Paul. Sienna? Why won't you answer me?" Trish drew her sweater across her chest. The temperature in the room seemed to plummet and, though her palms were wet with perspiration, she shook with the cold.

Slowly, she stepped from her boxed-in hideaway, glancing to her right and left. In front of her on the floor was the cordless phone. It continued to ring.

Looking back over her shoulder, she moved toward the phone, picked it up, and pressed talk.

"Hello?" she whispered.

"Oh, Trish, I'm so glad I finally reached you. This is Margo from the nursing home. When you didn't come this morning, we got worried."

Trish looked at her watch. It was already eleven. She was supposed to be at the nursing home by ten.

"Trish, are you there?"

"Yes." Struggling to bring her thoughts and emotions into alignment, she repeated a little louder, "Yes." She spun back around to face the mass of boxes and did a double, then triple take, on the entire room. There was no sign of anyone.

"Are you okay?"

"I'm sorry, Margo," Trish held the phone in her right hand and stared down at the spot of blood blazing on the Kleenex. "I had a little accident," she tried to explain. "I . . . cut my finger."

"Oh, Trish. I'm so sorry. Is it serious?"

"Ah . . . no." Trish continued speaking, her voice still low and guarded as she walked back over the floor above Sienna's room and the guest room. Her entire body seemed to pound with the beat of her heart. If someone were there—someone besides Paul or Sienna—it would be best that she be on the phone with Margo so the woman could summon help.

"I think I've got the bleeding almost under control. I'm . . ." Trish took one big step forward and turned quickly to her right, fully expecting to find someone there.

The attic was empty.

A rush of air escaped Trish's mouth in a relieved puff. "I'm sorry, Margo, why did you say you were calling?"

"Dear, do you remember the man in room thirty-seven? His name is Randall. He hasn't been feeling well—he hasn't been able to shake a cold. Well, the doctor just left. It's pneumonia. He doesn't think Randall has much time, maybe only a few hours."

"Can't they get him to the hospital?"

"He refuses to go. Says all he wants to do is talk to you. And there was something about a person named Luca."

"He *says?* Margo, what do you mean? I thought the man in room thirty-seven lost his ability to talk when he had his stroke."

"That's what we all thought. But first thing this morning he started saying your name and made it plain he has to talk to you."

"The nurses said he wanted to be left alone," Trish said. "The only time I've seen him was as they wheeled him up and down the hall to and from meals. Margo, I don't even know him. Why does he want to talk to me?"

***

WHEN SHE WALKED INTO ROOM thirty-seven, Trish saw that an oxygen mask had been placed on the tall, thin man lying in the bed. She judged him to be in his late sixties. Not endowed with the typical grandfatherly look of most men his age, he appeared, rather, to be a teenager who'd aged very quickly. His hair, black but now peppered gray, was full, with no signs of thinning. His skin was pulled taut over his bony frame and, except for three deep vertical wrinkles between his eyebrows, his face was plain and expressionless. Sallow circles had formed beneath his eyes, the result, one of the nurses once said, of years of hard living and hard drinking.

The man's eyes were closed, and for a moment she thought she was too late. As she studied his ashen face, she felt immediate guilt for what she'd been thinking earlier—that giving up and running away was her only option. Even with her future looming so uncertain, even with her family gone, compared to this poor man, she had everything.

She walked to his side and touched his hand then whispered, "Hello?"

His pale blue eyes opened.

"Oh." Trish smiled down at him. "Mr. . . . ." She realized she didn't know his last name. "I'm Trish Ingram. They said you needed to talk to me. What can I do for you?"

"Tah . . . rish." His mouth formed her name under the oxygen mask. "Tah . . . rish. Lu . . . . Lu . . . kuh." A mist of condensation formed on the inside of the mask with the old man's labored effort.

He turned his eyes away from Trish toward a small metal table next to the bed.

"I'm sorry, sir. I don't understand what you're trying to say."

"Lu . . . kuh . . . six." The word *six* seemed much easier for him to say than the first word he'd attempted.

"Six. You said six, right?"

He closed his eyes firmly then reopened them and looked straight at her as if to say that she was right.

"Okay, six. And Lu . . ." Trish fixed her gaze on the table the man kept staring at. It seemed there was something there he wanted her to know about. The makeshift nightstand held a plastic mug full of ice water with the name Randall C. written on the lid in black marker, a basin, and a Bible. *The Bible*. Was that it?

"Luke—did you say Luke? Luke chapter six?"

Again, he closed his eyes once.

Trish picked up the Bible and turned to Luke. "Which verse?"

"Three . . . six."

"Thirty-six? Is that it?"

Again, he gave a single blink.

Trish picked up the Bible, turned to the chapter and verse, and read it aloud.

"Luke chapter 6, verse 36: '*Be ye therefore merciful, as your Father also is merciful.*'" Trish paused and studied the man's face.

"Sev . . . en."

She looked back at the Bible and continued to verse 37: "'*Judge not, and ye shall not be judged; condemn not, and ye shall not be condemned: forgive, and ye shall be forgiven.*'"

Judge not . . . condemn not . . . forgive. The words echoed inside Trish's head. She looked down at the man. He blinked his eyes once and gave a slight nod.

"Ce . . . cile . . . for. . . give."

Trish nearly dropped the Bible. "Cecile?" The familiar name sounded strange to her as it escaped her lips. She realized that she'd never before said it aloud, at least not that she could remember. "Sir . . . *Randall* . . . how do you know about Cecile?"

Randall's only response was an unblinking stare. His eyes seemed to pierce her.

Her thoughts raced. "Cecile is—was—my *mother.* Randall . . . did you know her?"

"For . . . give," Randall repeated, then closed his eyes.

"Sir—you've got to tell me what you know about Cecile."

Margo appeared at Trish's side. "I'm sorry, dear." She gently grasped Trish's arm. "We need to let him rest."

"But I need to know . . ." Trish started to protest then realized Margo was right. Besides, it was probably only a coincidence—wasn't it? He knew a Cecile, but that didn't mean it was her mother. Still—tiny bursts of electricity ignited under Trish's skin, causing goose bumps to form on her arms—he'd said "forgive." Why would he want her to forgive another Cecile? Why had he wanted to talk to *her* in the first place?

The pages of the Bible fluttered shut as Trish closed the front cover. The action dislodged a small piece of cracked old paper that dropped to the floor. She bent down to retrieve it and, turning it over, saw that it wasn't paper at all. It was a photo of a very young woman with straight hair. She wore a long white coat.

***

BIKERS FOR FAMILIES WAS A nonprofit organization whose members came from all walks of life. Professionals and blue-collar workers alike, the people who comprised the group had one goal in common: aiding children who had lost one or, in some cases, both parents to drug abuse. Since the Christmas season was a particularly rough time for such children, the members of the northern Utah branch of the group planned to assemble that weekend on their motorcycles to visit several kids in the area and take them gifts. They'd ended up getting together sooner than anticipated. Paul gathered his fellow bikers for another mission—to help find Sienna.

After he'd sent a plea for help, Paul went to the house to find Trish. He intended to tell her that no matter how bad things were between them, they needed to combine forces to find their daughter. He'd been worried about her as well, but on the way there, he'd tried to convince himself that it wasn't unusual for her to be gone or unresponsive to his calls—especially after the messages he'd left for her telling her he was leaving. But when he arrived, he found something that alarmed him.

The house was in shambles.

In the middle of the family room floor, over half the decorations from the tree lay scattered about and broken. Numerous other holiday adornments had been wrenched from their places as well. Paul felt his chest tighten in concern as he viewed the signs of what looked like a mighty struggle—but between whom? And where was Trish? Was she okay?

Stan Crawford, a local lawyer and member of Bikers for Families, walked up behind Paul as he looked at the debris strewn across the floor. He put a hand on Paul's shoulder. "It's not likely any bad guy is going to stop and bother to take down the Christmas decorations. So, chances are, there wasn't some kind of maniac here assailing your wife."

Paul held his cell phone up to his ear. He'd tried repeatedly to call Trish on hers. Still no answer. He turned down the hallway and ascended the stairs two at a time, followed by Stan. The two men stepped to the end of the bed. There, in a tangled pile on the floor, were several items of clothing belonging to Trish.

"These are soaking wet . . ." On impulse, He darted to Sienna's room. There, on the nightstand, was her cellphone. He picked it up. The battery was dead. How did it get there? She hadn't even been inside when he'd been dropped off. Paul's thoughts were interrupted by the sound of Mike's voice downstairs.

"Paul, come here!"

He responded to the urgent tone in his brother's voice, descending the stairway the same way he'd gone up, taking the steps two at a time.

"Look at this," Mike said.

Mike had been assisting the bikers set up a sort of command post. They'd spread out a map of the area in the garage and, as they'd each arrived or called to report the areas they'd searched for Sienna, Mike marked off the roads with a yellow marker. Paul had suggested they take the effort into the house to get out of the cold.

Now he walked toward Mike in the kitchen. Yellow marker in one hand, Mike pointed to spots of red on the breakfast bar.

Blood.

Paul followed the trail to the breakfast nook and out to the family room. The drops convinced him that Trish was in some kind of trouble. He looked from Stan to Mike. Apprehension filled their faces. Stan pulled a cell phone from his shirt pocket.

"I'm going to call Sergeant Connolly, tell him we're looking for two women," Stan said.

Paul's jaw tightened as he listened to Stan speak to the sergeant.

"Yes, Sergeant, this is Stan Crawford. We're at Mr. Ingram's house and . . . what? They have? We'll be right there." Stan flipped his phone shut and jammed it back into his pocket. "Paul, come on. They've found something back down in Perry."

***

THE SCENE ON THE HIGHWAY was chaotic. When Paul pulled up on the Harley with Mike on the back, more than a dozen people—bikers who'd taken the day off work as well as law enforcement personnel—swarmed down a short, snow-covered embankment to the orchard below.

Dismounting the Harley, Paul was met by the sergeant.

"Mr. Ingram, one of your bikers was driving along in the emergency lane checking the area one more time when he caught a glimpse of red and decided to see what it was. We've dug the car out, but . . ."

Paul barreled past the officer and waded through the snow down the bank.

"Mr. Ingram . . ."

A couple of snow shovels were flung on the ground next to Sienna's Honda. Paul floundered over them to the side of the car and looked inside. "Where is she?" he yelled to no one in particular. "Did they already take her to the hospital?"

"Mr. Ingram," the sergeant caught up with Paul. "Mr. Ingram, that's what I've been trying to tell you. She's not here. The car was empty when we uncovered it."

CHAPTER 16

ONCE A RAUCOUS RAILROAD CITY on the transcontinental rail line, Corinne, Utah—nearly a century and a half later—was a placid, rural community where nothing much happened. But for Trish, the town was anything but serene; it was the core of raw anguish, the horrible stage on which the melodrama of her life had gotten its start. The town seemed to pulsate with an indescribable pain that seared into her heart as hot and real in the cold December afternoon as it had during her turbulent years as a teenager.

Steering the Miata off Highway 13 and onto a narrow country road, Trish drove past the post office and an ornate building with a sign in front proclaiming it to be the oldest existing Protestant church in Utah. Turning west, she maneuvered through an obstacle course of potholes and drove to the southwest edge of town, where a few pine trees lined the pavement alongside a chain-link fence. Two short, graveled lanes branched off the main road to her left. She continued to a third lane which passed beneath an arch supported by two rock pillars. Inside the arch, metal letters spelled out Corinne City Cemetery.

Though obviously plowed since last night's big storm, the lane she chose was still dotted with patches of snow. Trish drove too fast as she neared the end of it. The rear tires of the Miata spun, sending the car sliding sideways into a snow bank. Pulling the gear shift into reverse, she attempted to back out of the snow. The tires only spun deeper. She tried again. Shifting the car into drive, then reverse, she rocked it forward and back. The tires emitted a high-pitched whine.

She was stuck.

When she opened the driver's side door and stepped out, Trish quickly surveyed her surroundings. In the distance to the southeast of the cemetery were hundreds of black-and-white Guernsey milk cows belonging to the Campion family. Trish had been to the Campion Dairy many times in her youth. The huge milking operation was situated in the middle of nearly fifty acres of land. On the east edge of the property, surrounded by meticulously landscaped grounds that bordered the west bank of the Bear River, sprawled the Campion family home. Trish stiffened at the thought of Lynette. Though she'd married a wealthy film producer, the woman had retained her maiden name. And after he had passed away, she had moved back to care for her ailing mother. One of her sons now ran the dairy.

The north and east sides of the cemetery were bordered by fields. There were no other homes around for miles except for a small, run-down basement house barely visible on the west behind a burgeoning, six-foot-high hedge.

After walking a few paces down the lane, Trish stepped off into the snow and trudged toward the southwest side of the cemetery. Her calf-high snow boots quickly filled with snow, but she continued, determined to find her mother's grave.

On her left, by the small tool shed where lawn mowers were stored for the winter, a flag atop a tall pole rippled with the mild afternoon breeze. Every now and again, the breeze would gust harder for a moment, dislodging little clumps of snow that clung tenaciously to the now leaf-barren branches of the hedge.

Trish sidestepped past a deep snowdrift mounded around a couple of medium height headstones before arriving near the place where she thought her mother's grave was located. It had been nearly twenty-five years since she'd been to the cemetery. Now there were numerous additional graves, and the lawn, covered with snow, looked much different. The headstone on the grave was flat. Locating it under so much snow would be a difficult task.

Deciding she'd gone too far south, Trish turned back the way she came. She moved a few paces left then walked north, parallel with the hedge. If it hadn't been for a small potted Christmas tree, now half buried in the snow next to the headstone she sought, and had she not looked down to take note of the angel decorations on the tree, Trish might have missed her mother's grave altogether.

Before she got out of the car, she had removed her gloves from the pocket of her black wool coat. Pulling them on, she wished she'd brought the coat along as well. In a gesture of goodwill, she stooped to pick up one of the gold angel ornaments that lay a few inches away from the little two-foot-high blue spruce. She brushed the snow from the glass ornament with her fingertips and studied it as it lay cupped in her hands.

It looked identical to ornaments she had at home.

She laid the ornament aside, swept the snow from the branches of the tree, and moved the small mountain of drifted white that held it captive. Digging the snow away from the flat, rectangular stone next to the tree, she stopped and caught her breath. There it was—the headstone in the photo from the envelope. Her mother's headstone.

Her mother's grave.

Emotion surged through her body. The muscles in her stomach grew taut, and she clenched her teeth. She felt as though she had just laid bare all the horrors, anger, and madness of her life. She forced herself to read the words etched into the gray-brown stone. They were short and to the point:

> *Cecile Ann Anderson*
> *Born 1947*
> *Died 1970*

There was nothing else. No month or day of her birth. No note of her parentage. No mention that she was a mother. Just a brief, terse blurb indicating she'd spent a mere twenty-three years on the earth.

Trish mechanically picked up the fallen angel and placed it on the little tree with the others. As she completed the action a human voice sent pinpricks of shock through her body.

"Heard your tires spinnin'. Figured I'd better come see what the commotion was all about."

Trish stood and whirled around. A very tall, very old woman stood several feet away on the gravel lane. Unremarkable in her manner and dress, the woman's white hair was pulled back into a bun at the nape of her neck. Her face was as weathered as a piece of old barn wood. Her bare, gnarled hands were on her hips.

"The rest of 'em are over there. Shame they aren't all t'gether."

The woman wore a cotton housedress, blue with small white flowers, that flapped around her painfully thin legs in the breeze. Though the sun warmed the early afternoon, the fabric of the dress and the near-threadbare blue sweater the woman had on were not appropriate for the month of December. Yet, if the woman was cold, she didn't show any signs she felt it.

She had a worn but clean yellow apron tied around her waist, and her feet were clad in heavy looking dusky brown patent leather shoes, the tops of which were caked with snow. Despite her appearance, something about the woman's nature and the way she carried herself commanded attention.

"Margaret is with her parents." Drawing her right hand up slowly from her hip and pointing a long, bony finger to the grave at Trish's feet, she added, "Cecile should've been there, too. But the notions folks get into their heads—well, ya never know what they're a gonna do."

Trish was so preoccupied with the woman's clothes—worrying if she wasn't horribly cold—and wondering where she'd come from that she hadn't yet paid any attention to her words.

"Margaret?" The name struck a chord. Wiping a few stray crystals of snow from her gloves, Trish sorted through the bits and pieces of information stashed deep in the recesses of her brain. She shivered. She knew who Margaret was. She had to see if the woman really knew as well. "Who was Margaret?"

The woman's tone was slow and even. "Why, Margaret was Cecile and Kate's younger sister. That would've made her yer aunt."

Feeling unexpectedly vulnerable and exposed, Trish quickly scanned the rest of the cemetery to see if any additional locals had wandered in. Save for herself, the woman, and dozens of graves, it was empty. "How do you know that? How do you know who I am?"

The woman continued speaking as though she hadn't heard Trish's question.

"Yer girl was here yesterday. Put the tree on the grave. Decorated it right nice. It's a good thing, rememberin' the dead; they have a lot to teach. Too bad folks don't pay as much heed to 'em when they're livin'."

Sienna had been here?

No wonder the angel ornaments looked familiar—they were from a box of old decorations Trish hadn't used in years. Why had Sienna taken them? Why had she ornamented the little blue spruce and left it on her grandmother's grave? Trish's hands flew to her mouth. She suppressed a cry. Of course. The letter. Whoever had given it to Sienna had told her everything—right down to the last, sordid detail of her lineage.

Leaving the grave, Trish made her way through the snow to the lane. She stopped a few feet away from the woman, her heart thumping.

The woman turned away and gestured across the lane to the east. "That's where Rand will rest, with me and Charlie and Thomas. Yer girl put a tree there, too. Mighty nice a' her. Mighty good child she is."

Trish looked over to where the woman pointed and saw a grouping of weathered headstones and a single white metal cross. At its base was a small potted Christmas tree like the one on Cecile's grave. The woman turned back to face her. Trish stared hard at her, stunned at the old lady's seeming familiarity with her family and confused as to why Sienna would be concerned with the grave site of strangers. Who was this woman, and who were the people she mentioned?

Trish masked her fear and confusion with the resolve to comprehend what was unfolding. "How is it you know Sienna?" she asked, measuring her words with wariness. "How do you know me? Who are you?"

All that registered on the woman's face was a blank stare.

Trish tried again. "Let's start over . . . you said something about Margaret."

"Yes." The woman nodded. "There's Margaret, with Herb and Millie." She again turned away from Trish and pointed to two tall headstones at the side of the lane, a few rows north.

Shoving her hands into her pockets, Trish silently walked the
few yards to the graves. She could hear the woman shuffling along
behind her. Arriving at the tall columnar headstones that rose up
several feet out of the snow, Trish saw that a lamb was etched into
the white marble of the first one, along with ornate words:

> *Margaret Louise Anderson*
> *Our little joy*
> *Born September 21, 1951*
> *Torn from the arms of her loving mother, July 9, 1961*

A foot away, the second headstone was identical to the first,
except for the information etched into the marble. Two people
were buried here. Trish drew in a sharp breath as she recognized
the names of her mother's parents:

> *Herbert Marshall Anderson*
> *Born into the world August 2, 1918*
> *Died November 27, 1961, of grief*

> *Millicent Petersen Anderson*
> *Born May 22, 1922*
> *Died January 7, 1995*
> *Beloved mother of Margaret Louise Anderson*

"Herbert and Millicent!"

"Yes, Herb and Millie," the old woman, now standing at Trish's
side, asserted.

"Why doesn't it list Kate and Cecile?" Trish asked, her voice
strained. "They were her daughters too."

Several seconds passed before the woman spoke. Her tone was
soft and sounded mournful. "Folks are funny. Think they'll do
the Lord's business for Him, judge and condemn who they will.
Problem is, they don't know the heart like He does. He's the only
one who really knows any being." The woman shook her head.
"Yer grandmother made it clear neither yer mother's name nor yer
Aunt Kate's was to be on 'er headstone. It was one of the ways she

punished yer Aunt Kate for takin' yer mother's side in things, one of the ways she punished yer mother for the accident and all that happened after it."

"Accident . . . what accident?"

"Summer of 1961, and yer mama was just about the purtiest girl 'round these parts. No shame in that, but Millie never put much stock in purtiness nor all the boys hangin' round to catch a glimpse of her daughter. I'd better back up a ways, start at the beginin'. Ya see, Millie'd lost one baby after Kate was born. Then she had Cecile. Lost two more before Margaret—birthin' Margaret nearly took 'er life—but, oh, how Herb and Millie loved that child—'twas their miracle baby, they said.

"Times were hard. When Margaret came along, times got even harder, what, with another mouth to feed. Kate married five years later, and after she was gone, Herb and Millie 'spected Cecile to be a mama and a daddy to Margaret while they worked the farm. Oh, she did a good job of it, all right, for a girl her age, and no one can fault 'er for wantin' some time to herself that day. Back to 1961 . . . yes ma'am, I reckon all Cecile wanted to do was have a bit of time away from her little sister and the farm, go with her friends down ta the river."

"But the accident . . ." Trish pressed.

The woman looked Trish square in the eye. "Margaret followed Cecile and her friends. The older kids, they were all good swimmers, swam right out across the river to the other side. Margaret, bein' nine years old, probably convinced herself she wasn't gonna be ditched and thought she'd follow 'em. She didn't make it."

"Didn't make it?" Trish echoed the words. The breeze that played on the hedges and rippled the flag fell still as though, it too, was intent on hearing the woman's account.

"They found Margaret's body later that day. She'd gotten tangled in some branches somebody'd thrown in. Yer mother was all et up with guilt. Why, any soul could see she paid the price for what she'd done. Any soul, that is, 'cept yer grandmother. She worked it into yer grandpa's head that they had one dead girl and one who was no more than a murderer. Folks said he couldn't bear the burden of it." The woman's voice fell silent. She turned and began plodding slowly away, back toward the main road.

It took a few moments before the woman's words fully hit Trish. The part in her mother's letter she hadn't understood—*the lives I was responsible for ending . . .* The meaning of the words began to make sense. Trish took her hands from her pockets and firmly pressed them against her lips. This was a piece of her life's puzzle she had no idea existed. Cecile—her mother—had been the unwitting cause of her own sister's death and had borne the burden of blame and guilt . . . *No one understands the burdens that crush me . . .* Trish had known Margaret died young, but she never knew how. She never knew about . . . the accident. She never knew her mother's father had died just months later.

A tear made its way unchecked down Trish's cheek. For the entirety of her life, she'd felt nothing but contempt for her mother and what she perceived as Cecile's selfish actions. She'd had no idea that . . . Through a blur of tears, she saw the old woman moving farther away from her. "Wait!" Trish called out. "Is that all you know?" Rushing to the woman's side, Trish reached out and grasped her hands. "What happened then? Herbert's headstone said he died of grief. Was that because of Margaret's drowning?"

The old woman's lips formed a half smile. "You're gonna take a chill, child. Let's go back to the house."

***

What language was spoken in heaven?

Sienna didn't know, but it sure sounded like Spanish. She tried to shift her body, but her arms and legs were heavy and unresponsive. Her ears were the only things that seemed to cooperate with her brain. She tuned into the sounds she'd heard a few minutes ago—voices. Yes, there were voices. But what were they saying?

"*Rogelio, por favor, abre la puerta. Gracias. Ven y ayúdame, hijo. Pon la tazon a la boca de ella. Ella se debe comer.*" The words were spoken by a woman.

A young boy replied, "*Si, madre. Yo le ayudaré. ¿Se recuperará la muchacha?*"

Sienna was certain the people were talking about her. But what were they doing, and where was she? Someone gently caressed her forehead. The woman spoke again.

"*Cóme, muchacha. Te necesitas comer para recuperar la fuerza. Rogelio, cómo se dice comer en Inglés?*"

"Eat, Mama. Eat. Yes, she needs to get her strength now," the boy responded.

Sienna felt a hand at the back of neck; it gently lifted her head up a few inches.

She felt something hard pressed against her lips. A trickle of warm liquid was poured into her mouth. She swallowed then coughed.

"*Sí*, eat. Eat." the woman said softly.

The broth tasted salty and good. Sienna swallowed one mouthful, then a second and a third. She licked her lips and moved them slightly to make sure she had command of them before she tried speak. "Telephone. I . . . I need a telephone."

"*Rogelio, qué dijo la muchacha?*"

"*Un teléfono, Mamá. Ella quiere llamar a alguien* . . . She wants to call someone."

CHAPTER 17

TRISH FOLLOWED THE OLD woman down six crumbling steps into the basement house west of the cemetery. As she did so, an ugly tide of shame washed over her. She'd been so immersed in misery that she hadn't paid heed to common sense. The woman couldn't have appeared out of nowhere, and there were no other houses around for miles—except for the basement house. Ever since she could remember, it had belonged to only one family—the Clarks.

The woman must be Bessie Clark.

At the bottom of the stairs was a shabby wooden door, aged and weathered from years of use. A red felt bow hung suspended on it from a piece of rusty wire. Bessie opened the door by simultaneously turning the handle, pushing it with her right foot, and giving it a shove with her right shoulder.

Immediately inside the door was the kitchen. Cramped and dimly lit, its bare cement walls, as evidenced by faded and peeling patches of paint, had long ago born an effervescent shade of blue. Trish couldn't help but compare the walls to Bessie. The Bessie Trish remembered from her childhood had been a striking woman who always held her head high. Trish remembered seeing her walking into town to purchase groceries or attend church on several occasions. Her long black hair was always well kept. Her clothing, though far from fashionable, was always neat and pressed, and she possessed an air—a vibrancy—that made others turn and look her way.

Now, like the paint on the walls, most of that vibrancy had faded from Bessie, yet hints of it remained in the way she carried herself and in the graceful gestures of her hands despite their aged and arthritic condition.

Trish's sense of shame increased. Bessie had always been poor—desperately poor—and the object of much mockery. Trish sighed sharply and dropped her chin toward her chest as she studied the woman who busied herself at the ancient wood cookstove tucked against the east wall of the kitchen. It was no wonder she remembered Trish—Bessie had once been the object of *her* ridicule.

"Take them boots off and put 'em over here by the stove," Bessie commanded.

Trish obliged. Setting the boots next to the old cook stove and removing her gloves and sweater, she warmed herself before the old woman motioned for her to sit at a tiny table. Rimmed by silver-colored metal bearing small spots of rust, the table had a gray Formica top supported by metal legs. Two matching chairs with metal legs and cracked yellow vinyl backs and seats were placed on either side. Trish chose the chair by a small window near the top of the wall and sat down.

From where she positioned herself, Trish could view almost the entire home. It shocked her to think that a house the size of Bessie's would easily fit inside her family room with space to spare. How had the woman survived here all these years?

In the southwest corner of the house was a living room. Not a quarter of the size of Trish's bedroom, the room hosted a small wood-burning stove, a rocking chair, and a small green sofa that had definitely seen better days, an old treadle sewing machine, and a needle-bare Christmas tree. Despite surroundings that spoke of a penury Trish couldn't even begin to comprehend, Bessie seemed to be in her element.

As the old woman bustled about the little kitchen, heating water on a stove that gleaned its temperature from wood instead of electricity, getting cups from a cupboard that had no doors, and putting cookies onto a blue tin plate, she literally glowed. She'd retied her apron, straightened her shoulders—which were not stooped and bent like those of most women her age—and she'd begun to hum. In this, her own little piece of the universe, far removed from the world, Bessie Clark was the very picture of contentment.

Trish felt a pang of envy.

Looking up, she saw a picture of Christ hanging just above the table. He smiled down on the kitchen. He smiled down at Trish. She caught herself smiling back. At the edge of the table, next to the wall, was a Bible. Trish ran her fingers over the worn front cover, suddenly remembering what had happened with Randall, suddenly remembering why she'd come to Corinne. That would have to wait. She had at least a dozen questions for Bessie, but first she needed to get something else out of the way.

Bessie approached the table with two cups of steaming hot cocoa and placed one in front of Trish. She sipped from the other cup and advised, "I make it a mite strong. Let me know if it doesn't suit you."

After tasting the cocoa, Trish said, "It's very good. Thank you." She set her cup down and folded her arms in front of her. "I'm sorry I didn't recognize you earlier. I remember now—you're Bessie Clark."

Bessie sat her cup down on the table and turned back toward the stove. Her hands moved deftly, transferring an old copper teapot to a front burner, then removing a back burner—a disk of cast iron that she lifted up with a handle fashioned of the same—in order to add another stick of wood to the fire that blazed inside the stove. A marvel in and of itself, the old stove was plated with white porcelain and appeared to have two ovens. A built-in thermometer on one of the oven doors showed the temperature. Bessie noticed Trish studying it.

"There's a knack to it," she said. "When Charlie first brought it home from his mother's house, I burned nearly everythin' I put into it. Took me fifty-odd years to get some things right. Now, it purty near runs itself. Helps that the cook's gotten smarter too." Bessie smiled broadly and winked at Trish. "Just made these this mornin'. Try one."

She set a plateful of molasses cookies down in the center of the table. Remembering she hadn't eaten a thing all day, Trish helped herself to two of them. Bessie settled onto the other chair. They both sipped their cocoa and nibbled their cookies in silence. Somewhere in the living room, a clock ticked the seconds by.

After wiping her mouth on the corner of a paper napkin, dotted with blue snowflakes and looking like it had been purchased at least a decade before, Trish cleared her throat. "Bessie, I . . . I owe you an apology."

"Don't know what for," Bessie said matter-of-factly.

Trish laid the napkin on the table. "Years ago, I was one of a bunch of kids that egged your house. I'm sorry. I truly am. Then . . ." The next revelation wasn't as easy to speak about. "Then, once when you were walking home from town, I threw a tomato at you. I was riding in Lynette Campion's car, and she dared me to do it." Trish quickly added, "That's no excuse—I knew better. And I . . . called you a witch. I wasn't very nice back then."

Bessie finished her cocoa and put her cup down on the table. "Figured that mighta been you," was all she said.

Trish shifted uncomfortably on the chair. She tried again. "I've made a lot of changes. I'm trying to be a better person. At least that's what I've been telling myself . . ." She added the last part, remembering that her husband and only child couldn't stand to be near her anymore and that only hours ago she'd been steeped in such torment she'd ripped down all the Christmas decorations in her home.

Trish took stock of her surroundings once more and swallowed hard. Save for three Christmas cards taped to the front of a sputtering old refrigerator between the stove and sink, the tree in the living room, and the red bow on the door, Bessie had no such luxury as Christmas decorations.

Bessie broke the awkward silence. "Used to tell my boy there's only two folks ya gotta worry about—Him," Bessie pointed up to the picture of Christ, "and yerself. Long as things are right with those two, everything else'll follow after."

"I wish it were that easy," Trish stammered, inadvertently clunking her cup down a little too hard on the table. "People expect things of you. They expect you to be a certain way—act and dress in a certain manner—in order for them to accept you."

Bessie seemed to ponder the opinion Trish laid out before her, then said, "I figure that's not why we're here. I must've read the Bible cover to cover a dozen times or so, and nowhere've I seen anything about havin' to be somethin' you're not just to please folks."

"It's just the way of the world," Trish tried explaining. "It's . . . it's . . ." She couldn't find the right words to explain her thoughts. Tears pushed at the edges of her eyelids. She'd fought all her life to escape what would have been her birthright: the daughter of—she forced herself to acknowledge it—an unknown father and an unwed mother who'd abandoned her by committing suicide, the object of pity for her aunt and uncle who'd taken her in as a foundling. Her only chance not to be a Bessie herself had been to claw her way up the social and economic ladders of the world.

As if reading her thoughts, Bessie interjected, "The Lord came into the world with nothin', and He left with nothin'—nothin' that would be of value to most folks. I guess I'll be doin' the same." Bessie folded her hands in her lap and leaned toward Trish. "But what He gave—*that* was what counted. I pray I can give it too."

Trish looked into the eyes of the Christ in the picture. What had He given? His life, yes, but what else? Her face felt hot, her hands clammy. Then she realized: it was exactly what Jamie had given and what Jamie had asked her to give—the Lord had given the gift. He'd given the gift of love.

Trish cleared her throat again as a wave of emotion threatened to rock her off-balance. She had to stay on course. "Bessie, please, tell me what happened to Cecile—to my mother—after Margaret died."

"Ya sure you want to know?"

The question caught Trish off guard. "Well . . . yes. Yes. You seem to know things about my family, and I . . . I need to know too. I've spent a long time running and . . ." She pushed the stray tendrils of her hair firmly behind her ears and whispered, "I'm tired of running. I've got nothing left to lose, really, and nowhere to go . . ."

Thinking of all that had transpired that day—reading the letter, wanting to succumb to her grief and run even farther away, convinced it was her only option, and then the phone mysteriously ending up on the floor of the attic, the call urging her to go to Randall's side, the scripture in Luke, and Randall's strange admonition—*forgive Cecile*—Trish added, "Something happened to me today. Actually, over the past year you wouldn't believe *all* that has happened. But today I had to make a choice. I thought it would be best if I just gave up . . . Then I got a call."

She caught her breath. "I don't even know how the phone ended up where it was. The important thing is I answered it and found out someone needed me—someone I didn't really even know—and I'm still not exactly sure why. When I got there I found more questions than answers, but I realized that no matter how bad things were, no matter how much pain I was in, I couldn't just quit. I had to try and have . . . faith. That's why I ended up in the cemetery. I'm trying to piece things together and have faith that I can figure things out."

Bessie didn't speak.

Trish went on. "The poor man I went to see at the nursing home where I volunteer on weekdays was so sick and probably not quite in his right mind. Or was he?" She shook her head. "I don't know. But there was this scripture about not judging or condemning, about forgiveness, and he said something . . . he said, 'Forgive Cecile.' I mean, I know it was only a coincidence, that there was someone he knew—another Cecile—he was talking about, trying to make amends with. But I thought, could it really be that simple?"

Her chin trembled. She wiped her nose on the paper napkin. "I'm sorry. I'm just babbling. I've fooled myself about a lot of things, and to go reading something into what that man said, well, it's plain stupid. The truth is, Bessie, I don't know how to change or to make anything any better. I'm the same horrible fool I was when I hung around with Lynette Campion. My sister-in-law, Jamie, told me to give the gift—the gift of love. I've tried so hard, but all I've managed to do is make a mess of things—my husband and daughter hate me, and I deserve it—I deserve everything I've gotten."

"Child, ya don't have to go on like yer mother." Bessie unfolded her hands and reached across the table to touch Trish's shoulder. "She tried all her life to please folks—yer Grandma Millie and Grandpa Herb, them in this town that scorned 'er for bein' who she was, and . . . she had a good heart. She just didn't know about those two most important people I told ya of: the Lord and herself. She didn't know He was a holdin' out His arms to her all along. All she had to do was love 'erself like He did, give what you call 'the gift' to 'erself. She didn't do it, but you can."

Trish looked deep into Bessie's eyes as her own misted with tears. She shook her head from side to side, then stood up too quickly from the table. Little spots of bright white light filled her vision. She stumbled forward.

Bessie rose to her feet and took hold of one of Trish's arms. "Trisha, the Lord is holdin' out the gift for ya now. Let yerself have it; love yerself like He does. Everything else'll fall into place. Forgive yourself, if needs be, and those others in your life who need forgivin'. Like Luke tells us in the Bible, *'Judge not, and ye shall not be judged; condemn not, and ye shall not be condemned . . .'"*

". . . forgive . . . and ye . . . shall be . . . forgiven." Trish choked back tears as she finished the scripture. It was the same one she'd read to Randall that morning. Loving and forgiving herself was a foreign, abstract concept she didn't know how to bring to fruition. Forgiving others—forgiving her mother—was something she was working on, but . . . *stay on course . . . stay in control.* Control. Now there was something she knew about.

Trish had to regain control.

Questions she'd had about Bessie and their conversation in the cemetery shot back into her heart like arrows. How did the old woman know so much about her, about her family? Sure, she lived in the same community they had, but her observations seemed much more than casual, like she'd made Trish's family the object of study. Why did she have such a strong interest?

"The fact is, my mother never even knew who my father was. I'll have to live with that forever. He could be anyone. That she didn't even know who he was, that she killed herself . . . that she quit and left me—a three-year-old—behind to deal with the consequences of her actions! I don't know how you know so much about my family, but if there's anything else you can tell me about my mother . . ." The foamy waters of despair and emotion surged with urgency around Trish's senses. Struggling for breath, she strode into the small living room, seeking air.

She had to have air. "As far as I can see, nothing, not even her guilt over her sister, excuses what she did to me. She left a letter behind. Today I read a part of it, but it's no excuse for what she did to *me*."

Bessie followed Trish into the living room.

"To you? Trisha, if ya have in yer mind yer mother didn't love you, let me tell ya—she did. I know she did. If she hadn't of, she wouldn't have tried so hard to make sure you'd be cared for when she left ya here that night, left that letter . . ."

Trish spun around to find Bessie in tears.

". . . I tried to get to 'er in time . . . ran all the way into town with you on my hip. Tried stoppin' at a few houses, but folks . . . folks wouldn't pay me no mind. So I kept goin'. Somethin' told me that's where she'd go—where Margaret died."

Her mind in a haze of shock and confusion, Trish began to stagger toward Bessie. "I was with you? What are you talking about? No. That can't be! She left me standing next to the Bear River Bridge when she jumped. I stood alone in the cold and watched my mother . . ."

Something caught Trish's eye.

On the north wall of the living room, the one wall she hadn't been able to see from the kitchen, stood an old upright piano. On top were several photographs and a nativity scene. Trish moved past Bessie and picked up one of the pieces from the nativity, a rock painted to resemble Mary, the mother of Christ.

"She painted that. Cecile was an artist, yes she was. If I recall, you should have one of those nativities yerself. I gave it to Kate to give to ya."

Gingerly, Trish set Mary back down as her eyes met those of a tall, thin man in one of the framed photos. He was young and, standing next to him, was a young Bessie.

Randall.

Another photo, this one unframed, was propped against the ticking clock. Though it was obviously of the same man, he appeared to be several years older than he was in the first photo. He stood next to a young woman in a long white coat. In his arms he held . . . a baby.

What was it Ann had said yesterday about puzzle pieces? Trish had just found an entire fistful. What would she do with them?

"This . . . is me," Trish offered, her head bobbing up and down, "the child in Randall's arms." She reached out to pluck the photo off the piano but quickly drew her hand back. "I know this is my mother. Is . . . is Randall my father?"

"No, child." Bessie guided her to the sofa then took the pictures from the piano and sat next to her. "Randall is my younger brother."

"Then who is my father? Do you know?"

Bessie rose and retrieved a framed photo of a teenage boy from the wall by the piano. "This is my Thomas just afore he went to Vietnam. He fell crazy in love with yer mother, summer of 1966. Was after he went back, she found out she was expectin' you." Bessie dried her tears from earlier with a plain white handkerchief. She folded the hankie and, hands in her lap, sat tall and proud on the sofa. "They say my boy was a hero. Stepped in front of a friend, took a single bullet. They gave him the Purple Heart."

"He died?"

"December 20, 1966—forty-one years ago yesterday. I didn't think yer mother'd be able to hold on, Thomas bein' the only person ever—'cept yer Aunt Kate—who took a notion to care about 'er. Yes, there's them that say Herb died of grief over Margaret, but if ya ask me, it was mostly Millie buildin' it up. Herb's heart wasn't good; think he woulda gone anyways. But Millie blamed your mother for Herb's death as well as Margaret's, and when she found out about Cecile bein' pregnant—on top of everythin' else she ever blamed the girl for—she 'bout went wild with anger. Locked yer mother in the shed fer a few days, I heard told. Yer mother wouldn't tell a soul who the father was. Never even knew myself. She didn't want to bring any disgrace on Thomas. Didn't want Millie draggin' him down as well."

Bessie rose and walked into another room. "Come on, child," she beckoned. "That night she brought you here—bein's as it was three years since his death—I finally was sure. I never told no soul, neither. But," she put a gnarled hand on Trish's arm. "I loved ya from afar, knowing that'd have to be the way things had to be."

Without conscious thought, Trish had risen from the sofa to follow the old woman. They were in a small bedroom now. "This was yer father's room, his things. This here's his ball glove—loved baseball, he did. This here poster of Willie Mays—one of the other boys in his unit sent it to me after he died. Here's Thomas in this photo Randall took before he left that fall. Here's him with yer mother."

Trish looked at the photos in stunned silence. "But the letter. You said she left it here the night she jumped. Did you read it?"

"Never opened it, child."

"But how did Sienna get it?"

"That ya'd have to ask yer Aunt Kate. I gave it to her, she bein' yer mama, then I figured she'd have to find a way, in her own due time, to tell ya everythin'. Gave her the nativity, a pretty rock Cecile'd painted like a swan for ya when ya was little, some photos, and . . ."

"And a pocket watch with the initials R.C.—Randall Clark."

"Yes. Some folks 'round here used to stop their clocks or watches when a loved'un died. Randall was there that night too. Stopped his watch, all right, by smashin' it on the corner of the bridge railin'. That was only after he'd jumped in his self and tried to find 'er. He didn't want to quit, thought he could save 'er. A couple of men from town pulled him thrashing from the water."

If Trish's heart was still beating in her chest, she couldn't feel it. Her words were more a rush of air than actual speech. "He's holding me in the picture on the piano. Did he know Thomas was my father?"

"Rand never was much fer words. But his heart," Bessie pointed to her chest, "he knew things in his heart. After my boy died and you was born, he put two and two together afore I ever did. Used to deliver milk 'round here, delivered it to Cecile, for ya when ya was a startin' to walk, at Millie's. Few things Cecile said, the look of ya—yer eyes like Thomas's—and he had it figured. That picture was taken May of 1968, yer first birthday. Yer Aunt Kate and yer mama was havin' a party for ya. Rand came 'round as usual that mornin' with the milk and asked to hold ya. Kate took a picture of the three of ya."

"How long has he been in the nursing home?"

"Goin' on ten years now. I visit him every Sunday morning. He's always had ill health since that night in the river." Bessie dropped her chin down and pursed her lips before adding, "That ya ended up in the same place where he was, I reckon that was a miracle of sorts."

Bessie's conclusion caused spirals of emotion to tingle through Trish's body. She nodded slowly, contemplating how many questions had been answered and how many more yet hung in the balance. "Bessie, did Kate know Thomas was my father?"

"I suspect she did, child, but I've told ya what I can of yer story, Trisha. Rest of it isn't rightly mine to tell. Kate made 'er decisions, had 'er own reasons for things—like other folks out here. Just like my sister, Ellie, and . . . those Campions."

***

SOMETHING SOFT NUZZLED SIENNA'S CHEEK. She opened her eyes in the bright afternoon sunlight to find a puppy next to her.

"*Señorita,* she likes you. She has no name yet, but she is yours. My gift to you. *Feliz Navidad.*"

Sienna looked up at a round-faced young boy, maybe nine or ten years old. She recognized his voice from earlier, bits of Spanish interlaced with his almost-fluent English.

"Where . . . am I?" Sienna managed to croak out.

"Here. Drink." He offered Sienna a glass of warm, bitter-tasting liquid before saying, "You are in our home, the home of the Reyes family. I am Rogelio."

Sienna took a drink from the glass. It seemed to sharpen her senses. "Where are your parents?" She struggled up on one elbow. "What day is it?" She pushed herself upright in the makeshift bed that sat on the floor of a room made from cinder block walls. "Do you have a telephone here? I need to call my father." The puppy whimpered and licked her hand. She nestled it in her lap.

"So many questions, *Señorita.* I will try to answer them. *Mi padre,* my father, has gone before us into heaven. Mama is resting in her room." The boy pointed toward the doorway. "She is very tired. She cared for you all through the night. As for the day, it is *Martes*—Tuesday. When I looked at the clock a minute ago, it said the time was three fifteen and, as for a telephone, I am sorry, but we do not have one."

"Tuesday. Three fifteen!" Sienna pressed the fingers of her right hand to her forehead then pushed her legs out from underneath the blankets, causing the puppy to whimper again. "I've got to find my dad."

"*Señorita,* Mama said I must get you to eat—for your strength. Here, eat this bowl of soup. It will be good for you. Then I will help you find your father."

Sienna considered the boy's words. She did feel weak and a bit light-headed. She accepted the soup and began to spoon it into her mouth. It was warm and spicy and contained bits of chicken and pieces of rice. When she finished, the boy went to the kitchen and refilled the bowl, returning it to her along with a couple of warm tortillas.

The sound of laughter shimmered into the room. Two little girls with shining black hair and large, beautiful brown eyes appeared in the doorway.

"*¡Cállete!*" The boy put his finger to his lips, then motioned for the girls to leave.

"It's okay." Sienna smiled. "Let them come in." Following a nod from the boy, the little girls ran into the room and tumbled onto the bed next to Sienna and the puppy.

"These are my sisters, Belicia and Calida," Rogelio announced.

Sienna finished the second bowl of soup as the girls petted the puppy. Though they coaxed, the dog had seemed to have formed a bond with Sienna. It refused to leave her lap.

"*Fedelina,*" the older of the two girls said to Sienna. "*Se la debe nombrar Fedelina a la perrita.*"

"What did she say?" Sienna asked Rogelio.

"She said you should name the puppy Fedelina. It means little faithful one." The boy's countenance took on a serious manner. "It was the dog's mother who found you."

"Her mother?" asked Sienna.

"Yes, *Anjelita.*"

The name sounded so beautiful when the boy pronounced it.

"Anjelita," Sienna repeated. "What does it mean?"

"It means . . . heavenly messenger," said Rogelio.

CHAPTER 18

January, 2010

THREE WEEKS HAD PASSED SINCE Jamie had appeared so suddenly at Trish's front door. It was ten PM, well after visiting hours, Paul was away on business, and finally—finally—Trish had worked up enough nerve to visit Jamie in the hospital.

"Get you anything?"

"No."

"More juice?"

"No, thanks."

Trish sat back on the edge of the chair next to the bed. A small bulletin board in the room displayed numerous cards, along with pictures of children and teens Trish didn't recognize.

"Thank you for coming, Trish. It means a lot."

"It was the least"—Trish's voice cracked—"I could do." She changed the subject. "Hey, who was the young woman with the short brown hair that was here a while ago?"

"Um, Lexie? Lexie Rogers, the director of the Providence Center. Trish, she's been gone for almost an hour. How did you know she was here?"

"I've been down the hall . . . for a little while."

"Down the hall?"

"Yes, until all your other visitors were gone."

"Trish, why didn't you just come on in while Lexie was here? It would've been okay."

"I didn't want to interrupt. Plus, I didn't want to give anybody too big of a shock, you know, snotty sister-in-law comes calling."

"You're not my snotty sister-in-law." Jamie looked at Trish and laughed. "At least not anymore. You're here, aren't you? If I thought you were still my snotty sister-in-law I'd have to call security. *'Nurse, we've got a code red. Rich lady with an expensive red cardigan and dyed-to-match shoes and handbag who won't crack a smile.'*"

"Jamie, how can you joke when . . ."

"When I'm on my deathbed?"

Trish abruptly rose from the chair and walked to the window.

"How can I not? I could just lie here watching reruns of corny soap operas and sitcoms, or I could have them turn off the lights and hang out the Do Not Disturb sign. But then I'd miss some really great stuff. I'd miss seeing Mike and holding his hand a few more times. I'd miss seeing my friends and hearing about how life goes on. I would have missed meeting Betty Carey."

"Betty Carey? Who's Betty Carey?"

"The nurse that came to hook up my new IV this afternoon. She's just a kid, really, in her early twenties. Her husband and twin sons—two-year-olds—were killed in a boating accident a few months ago. She doesn't need to work—his life insurance policy left her plenty—but she does because she enjoys working with the patients here in the unit. She said she likes trying to make their lives a little brighter." Jamie coughed and seemed to struggle for a breath.

Trish hurried over and put a paper cup full of apple juice into her hand. As Jamie sipped, Trish said, "You've had your share of heartaches too, Jamie. More than your share. But . . ."

"But what? Come on, Trish, spit it out. We're on a timetable here."

"Jamie . . . I go back and forth thinking you're so flippant to thinking you're so brave, and I'm not sure which one it is. I've always thought you just glided through life without taking things seriously—that you didn't care. But when you talk like you just did about the young nurse, Betty, I can see you do care. You care deeply. And you cared enough to come and see me a few weeks ago . . . So I guess what I don't understand is what lets you be so carefree. To be able to see the light side of things. For instance, you told me that day that Mike and Stephanie would be taken care of. How can you be so sure? When you're gone, they'll be alone. You don't know what's going to happen to them."

"Faith."

"Faith?"

"Yes, faith, Trish. Look it up in the dictionary. It means confidence or trust. I may not have been a church-lady type, but I do believe in God. I know He's there, and I have faith He'll take care of Mike and Stephanie."

Trish shook her head and pressed the fingers of one hand firmly against her mouth. She walked back to the window.

"It sounds so good, Jamie. But if He really cared wouldn't He just let you stay to raise Stephanie, at least until she's a teenager? I mean, she's already lost one mother. And Betty Carey—her two little boys . . . where are they now? Why wouldn't He let them stay with their mother? Babies like that belong with a mother."

Jamie pushed herself up on one elbow and fumbled with the controls on the bed that brought the back of it upright.

"Jamie, don't. Lie down. I'm sorry. I've said too much."

"No, Trish. You haven't. Do you know how long I've wanted to have this kind of discussion with you? How many times have I tried over the years to talk to you, and you've just shut me down? Well, this time you asked for it, and here it is, another word: *providence*. It means divine direction guiding the universe and the affairs of humankind with wise benevolence. It means we may not understand how God works but we can be assured of the truth that what He does is for our benefit. What's more is that He has angels, both in heaven and on the earth, who help Him help us. If I'm not here for Mike and Stephanie, I have faith that He will send someone to take care of them—I *know* He will, Trish. I have no doubt." Jamie coughed again and settled into her pillow.

Trish sat back on the edge of the chair, thinking again of the woman who had been there earlier. "You said something about that woman, Lexie. You said she worked for a center, a providence center. What is that?"

"*The* Providence Center. And she doesn't work there, she volunteers, like all the others. It's an after-school program for kids." Jamie looked at the bulletin board.

"These cards. Are they from those kids? Jamie, did you work there—volunteer there too?"

"I actually *started* the Providence Center, Trish. There wasn't anything like it when I was a kid. No place to go after school if you didn't have a place to go, if you know what I mean. I could see so many of Stephanie's friends and other kids around town who were struggling. I wanted to find a way to help give them a little something, to help them believe in themselves—to have faith. I wanted to be a part of that divine direction."

Trish studied the faces of the kids in the photos—boys and girls who looked like they were from a multitude of backgrounds. "I had no idea, no idea that you were doing something like this. What will happen to them now?"

"You still don't get it, do you? Lexie knows just what to do, and when she needs it, Heavenly Father will send someone to help. Things will work out. Maybe I'll even get to hang around—after—and help guide things in the right direction."

"Do you believe that?"

"Do you?"

***

December 21, 2010

IT WAS A LONG WALK back into town. Trish was glad she had grabbed her coat and purse from the car. When she'd left for the nursing home, she'd picked up her phone from out of the snow where she had dropped it the night before. It had been on the charger in her car while she was at Bessie's. She knew she needed to check her messages, but for now it just felt good to breathe the crisp December air and think.

A red sports car pulled alongside her as she walked up the road toward the more populated center of town. The driver of the car, wearing a green sequined sweater and adorned by a diamond necklace and earrings that seemed to rival the brightness of the sun at midday, leaned out the window.

"Well, well. Trish Ingram. What in the world brings you out to my neck of the woods?"

It was Lynette Campion.

Trish's body constricted with anxiety. She moved her lips into a pseudo smile. "My car got stuck in a bank . . . back there." She gestured vaguely, deliberately avoiding any mention of the cemetery. She tried to give a confident little laugh, meant to hide the fact she was in distress; it came out as more of a nervous chortle.

Lynette let her mouth fall open in mock concern as her eyes studied Trish intently, sizing her up the way an animal considered its prey. "Isn't it lucky for you *I* happened along to save the day?" Lynette smiled at her own reflection in the rearview mirror and patted her bleached-blond hair. "Why, honey, who'd think you'd be clear out here, walking, when you're due at the tabernacle soon?"

Trish jerked her wrist up to get a good look at her watch. Four thirty. The program. She'd lost all track of time—she needed to be at the tabernacle not one minute later than six. She tried to even out her breathing, casually folding her arms to give Lynette the impression she was in complete control.

Too late.

Lynette looked her up and down, taking in—Trish was certain—her red-rimmed eyes.

Lynette gave a little snort. "Have you decided not to put the kids from the Providence Center on stage after all?"

Trish didn't like Lynette's tone when she said the word *kids*—a few of the others involved in the planning of the program had hinted to Trish that Lynette had her reservations about them being involved. Over the years, her harsh demeanor had softened little, if any. Trish stuck out her chin and fought to regain an aura of composure.

"Not at all. I just had . . . a few errands to run and the car getting stuck, of course, was an obstacle that I . . ."

"Someone *is* coming to get you, *right?*"

Trish raised a shoulder, unsure of what to say.

"Jump in." Lynette motioned to the other seat in the sports car.

Letting herself in the passenger side door, Trish fell a little too heavily onto the black leather seat. She straightened and casually crossed her legs as though she didn't have a care in the world.

Lynette regarded Trish for a moment, raising one of her full black eyebrows, then pressed her foot on the accelerator. As the car sped forward, she began to punch the buttons on the car's radio.

"Can't stand any more of those sappy Christmas songs. They're getting on my nerves."

She selected an oldies station. Trish recognized the voice of fifties crooner Bobby Allen.

"You've got nothin' unless you've got love . . . You've got nothin' until someone cares."

Referring to the song, Lynette interjected, "Boy, isn't that the truth. Now, *who* exactly did you say was coming to help you? Oh, I know." She put the forefinger of her left hand to her lips. "It must be that handsome husband of yours. What's his name again?" She slowed the car at a stop sign and glanced over at Trish.

Trish managed to squeak out, "Paul."

"Paul. That's right. See him all over these days riding his Harley. What's up with that?" Lynette dropped her voice and muttered, "Some sort of midlife crisis, people are saying, or something else . . ."

Trish felt her face flush red.

"You've got nothin' unless you've got love . . . so get yourself a sweetheart who cares." The voice of Bobby Allen droned on.

"Oh, I wouldn't worry about it too much, dear. After all—what is it my father always said about you? Oh, yes. You can take the girl away from her roots but you can't take the roots away from the girl. Paul, he's a sharp man . . ."

Trish was speechless. Before she could catch herself, her arms flew into a protective position, folded tight across her stomach. Seeing her reaction, Lynette pressed further.

"Hmm. If your friends can't tell you, then who can? You know I've always been your friend, Trish. I have to say I admire that you've come as far as you have. Who'd ever think someone like you would be where you are now?" She held up her right hand as she came to a stop sign. "Don't worry, I won't tell anyone about your little walk down memory lane here. Your secrets are safe with me. They always have been."

"Secrets?" Trish mumbled.

"You know, after my father died and I came back out here to live with my mother, bless her heart, I decided to do a little remodeling. One of the first things I did was have an entire bank of windows put in on the west wall in the dining room. Why, now I can see clear over to the cemetery." Lynette's voice took on a sugary-sweet tone. "That's where your car is stuck, isn't it? What I can't figure out is why someone who has come as far as you would chance jeopardizing it all. What if someone had seen you, Trish?"

Lynette stopped the car at a second stop sign and left her foot on the brake. She turned in her seat and shook her right forefinger at Trish.

"I know what lengths you've gone to protect yourself all these years, but if you choose to throw it away now, well, I'm warning you, if anyone finds out who you really are . . . I've got a stake in this too. Even though my father is dead, the Campion name is well respected. I'm beginning to regret ever having told you anything about your past."

Trish looked at Lynette, stunned. "What are you talking about?"

"I know Bessie told you. Last year that sister-in-law of yours, Jamie, came snooping around, then yesterday, your daughter."

Trish decided to play along. "And . . . so what if Bessie did tell me?"

"My grandmother knew Thomas was your father."

Trish cocked her head. "So?"

Lynette waved her hand dramatically. "So she had the good sense to keep it to herself. She knew when she had a good thing going. She and Bessie and Randall came from nothing, but why air dirty laundry? When she married into the Campion family she promised my grandfather she'd never speak to her family again."

Trish's mouth felt dry. Her mind racing, she moistened her lips with her tongue before she spoke. "Your grandmother's name was Ellie, right?"

Lynette gave her a quizzical stare. Trish was afraid she wouldn't answer.

"Sharp as always," Lynette mumbled.

Lynette once again moved the car forward, accelerating toward Corinne. Trish watched her flip on her turn signal and begin to negotiate a left-hand turn. Unlike Bessie, who glowed with a spirit of peace and goodness, the only thing that emanated from Lynette was cold, hardhearted cruelty. Remembering the collage of Lynette photos taped to the dresser mirror in the attic, Trish ground her fingernails into her palms. *Lynette Campion* was the kind of woman she'd wanted to become? Lynette was her ideal of strength? Cruelty and shallowness came from weakness—not strength.

Trish wanted something more.

Bobby Allen brought the old song to a close. ". . . *You gotta have love.*"

A rush of warmth like Trish had never before experienced filled her heart, strengthening her resolve. *You gotta have love.* Paul and Sienna might not want her love, but she didn't have to look far to find somebody else—herself. Until Bessie said it, she'd never considered giving the gift to herself—but she could, couldn't she? Growing within her was the desire to believe the Lord loved her too. Didn't Bessie say those were the only two people to worry about—one's self and the Lord? Didn't she say everything else would fall into place? As Jamie had tried to teach her—*providence.*

"I've had a habit of making things more complex than they are," Trish began. "They were really quite simple. I never knew who my father was, and my mother committed suicide. Thanks to you and others like you, I thought that meant I was nothing. I was afraid people would judge me, that I wouldn't measure up to everyone else. I tried to run from my past. I even lied to my husband and daughter. I thought they could never understand how stupid and worthless I felt. I thought if I could just take matters into my own hands, I could create a new me. A me that was above reproach. A me no one could question or challenge. I forgot one important thing."

Lynette stopped the car. "What are you talking about?"

"Look in the rearview mirror again, Lynette. What do you see?" Trish didn't wait. "I used to think I wanted to be just like you—Lynette Campion, strong and successful and rich. I had myself convinced that was the only way to deal with all my hopelessness and anger—cover it up. Run from it. Hide. Now I see I *was* just like you."

"Get out of this car, Trish."

"Are you really happy, Lynette?"

"Are you crazy?"

"Look at yourself and ask are you happy?"

"I said get out of this car."

Undeterred, Trish kept speaking. "I finally realized that you might be successful and you might be rich, but you aren't strong, and you're far from happy. Otherwise, you wouldn't act the way you do. Anger and cruelty come from fear—take it from me—I know."

"Out of the car, Trish."

Plato.

Trish opened the door but continued. "You're fighting a battle, Lynette. I don't know all the details, but what I do know is that your Grandma Ellie came from a very poor family. Somehow she met and fell in love with one of the Campion boys. But marrying into such a family had its price—she had to renounce her own family. The same prejudice that flowed from your grandfather, who asked her to forget them, flowed to your father and to you."

Trish stood by the side of the car. "You said you've always known who my father was, yet for all you knew about my mother's suicide and Kate being my aunt, you never revealed it. I wonder why—surely it isn't your depth of compassion. Now I understand. You had a secret too. You were afraid if you told anyone that Thomas was my father, it might come back to haunt *you*. You were afraid someone might start wondering about things and discover that Ellie Campion was the sister of Bessie Clark, the poor backward woman who lives in a basement house at the edge of your property. You wanted to go far enough to give me a hard time—I can see now how the Campions must have hated the Clarks, and why—but you didn't want to risk revealing too much."

Lynette glared. "You're as crazy as your mother!"

"I won't be part of carrying on the anger between our families, Lynette." Trish's words were firm and steady. "I refuse. The important thing I've forgotten until today was faith. Faith that we all come to this world and face different trials for a reason. Faith that we can choose what we want to make of ourselves, for better or worse. Faith that we only need to strive to do our best. Faith that the Lord loves us for who we are. I learned that today from my grandmother." Referring to Bessie as her grandmother filled Trish with an unexpected sense of pride. "You're right; you can't take the roots out of the girl. I don't think I'd have it any other way."

The look of shock on Lynette's face was once again replaced with anger. "Well, well," she laughed, "you being out here is fitting, don't you think?" She pointed past Trish to something behind her. "Fitting indeed."

Trish looked to what Lynette was pointing at. Several blocks away, rising above the tendrils of mist curling off the water below, the dark gray girders of the Bear River Bridge looked haunting and forlorn. Trish caught her breath.

"What shall I tell everyone at the tabernacle?" Lynette asked. "That Corinne's 'finest daughter' has gone to join her aunt and mother?"

In a voice barely above a whisper, Trish said, "I'm giving you a gift, Lynette. I forgive you for all you've said these past years, and I give you my love."

**

SINCE BEFORE SUNRISE, ANN MCCLURE Robinson and her husband, Mark, had scoured every road in the area, assisting in the search for their niece. Early that afternoon, they'd received word her car had been found off the side of Highway 89, just a few miles from their house. But Sienna hadn't been in the car, and dozens of law-enforcement officers, family members, and biker friends of Sienna's father had not been able to locate her, despite a massive search effort that covered three counties.

Now Ann stood in the middle of the lane near the farmhouse she and Mark lived in with their three children, Sam, Sarah, and Sean. She exhaled deeply, her breath turning to steamy vapor as the chill of early evening crept in with the setting sun.

Paul had phoned just after the discovery of the empty car to say that Trish was missing as well. Ann's immediate reaction was that Trish, who was prone to mood shifts, was responsible for her own disappearance. Sienna, however, was another matter—she'd never just disappear on her own.

An uneasy sensation bristled along the length of Ann's arms. When Trish had phoned that morning, Ann had tried to interrupt her tirade to tell her that her daughter was missing. She hadn't been able to get a word in edgewise, and she had realized that Trish was so engrossed in feeling sorry for herself that attempting to engage her help in locating Sienna would be totally useless. When Paul called, she told him she had spoken to Trish earlier in the day. She'd chosen not to mention that Trish said she was seeking a lawyer—and a divorce.

Ann walked away from the farmhouse, which was nestled in the heart of the family peach orchards. A good, hearty stroll almost always helped her find solace. Whenever she was troubled, she would take to the lane, sometimes walking the two miles due east until it reached the highway. By the time she arrived back home, she usually felt refreshed and ready to tackle her problems head on.

But today she was overwhelmed with a deepening sense of despair that no walk would remedy. It wasn't just her worry laced with a growing alarm over the disappearance of her niece, it was her conviction that Trish was somehow to blame. As evidenced by the phone call, Trish was so filled with self-pity and anger over what she perceived as the deficits in her life, she barely noticed what was going on with anyone around her.

For years, Ann had tried to reach out to Trish, the cousin her parents had adopted as their own. Since Trish had first come to live with them, when Ann was seven and Trish no more than a toddler, she'd tried to make Trish feel a part of the family, tried to be a real sister to her.

For a time, it worked until Trish hit junior high and got thrown into a larger mix of kids; one in particular, a nasty-tempered girl from Corinne named Lynette Campion, who knew more about Trish than Trish knew about herself.

Ann's parents had faced a tough decision in raising their niece. Kate and John agonized over how much of the horrible drama they should reveal to Trish, and when they should reveal it. At the time Trish came to live with them, they'd lived hundreds of miles away from Utah in Colorado. Their son, Robert, was born when Trish was six and, before they knew it, the years had flown by, with Trish integrating so well into the McClure family it became easier and easier to convince themselves they should never reveal her past. They chose instead to continue the ruse that she was their own.

Ten years after Cecile's suicide, they moved back to Utah and into the farmhouse, so John could take over his parents' peach orchards. And when Trish, at the age of thirteen, entered junior high, she had the misfortune of meeting Lynette Campion and her gang of prissy, conceited friends. In the decade the family was in Colorado, the few people who had known the truth had either forgotten or were no longer concerned about Cecile Anderson and the daughter she'd left behind.

Everyone, that was, except Lynette Campion. Ann could never comprehend the girl's motive for being so ruthless.

She stopped walking. These past several years, she'd been quick to place blame on Trish for many things. She expected Trish would have healed by now from what had occurred in the past. Maybe that was expecting too much. If Trish had not found out the way she had that she was adopted and learned about the circumstances of her conception and her mother's suicide, would things have been different? If Kate and John had told her everything before Lynette had, would Trish still have been filled with so much anger?

Ann hated to try to second-guess her parents. They'd done the best they knew how. Kate's mother—Ann's grandmother, Millie—had been a heartless woman. She'd wanted nothing to do with Trish after Cecile had committed suicide. There'd been an awful battle when Kate had stepped in and finally gotten custody. Millie had wanted Trish to be put up for adoption outside the family. She never again spoke to Kate and never acknowledged any of her grandchildren. Ann remembered seeing her obituary in the newspaper in 1995. The features of her face—the hard vertical wrinkles etched above her upper lip and the crease between her eyebrows—spoke of a woman who had never given up her bitterness.

A chord of compassion tugged at Ann's heart. Just being involved in a small portion of the family drama and knowing her grandmother's feelings toward them was hard to deal with. How much more difficult must it have been for Trish? Ann knew it had been devastating for her to find out the details of her past from a person like Lynette Campion.

If only things had been different.

But they weren't.

Everyone faced challenges in their lives—everyone. What made Trish think her particular set of trials give her the license to be so cold-hearted and introverted? She could have tried to change her attitude, couldn't she? She had a loving family that would have done literally anything for her.

Ann shook her head. Now so much was on the line. If Trish had taken a firm hold of Jamie's advice and given the gift to those who already loved her, maybe Sienna would have been safe at home last night, not out driving during the storm. Then again, Ann conceded, it was totally feasible that Sienna's actions had nothing to do with Trish.

When she was almost to the highway, Ann turned back toward the farmhouse. After their earlier search efforts driving the roads in one of the farm trucks, Mark had dropped her back at the house a short while ago to fix dinner for the kids. With a casserole prepared and put in the oven to bake, she'd decided she needed a minute to try and get her thoughts together; to try and think where else Sienna might be, what might've happened to her. But she hadn't gained a thing. Her mind felt more muddled and confused than when she'd left the house.

The fact was, she loved Trish and never considered her as anything less than a sister. They were getting older; life was short. She wanted Trish to be a part of her life; she felt Trish needed her too. Try as she might, she just didn't know how to help. Trish could be so emotional, like this morning when she'd called wanting to find a lawyer so she could get a divorce from Paul. Ann barely had the chance to get a word in edgewise. That's the way it was, talking to Trish—like trying to communicate with a wild bird, preoccupied with preening its feathers, who pecked at you if you got too close.

Passing the narrow dirt road that branched north off the lane leading back to her house, Ann noticed the persistent barking of a dog. She stopped and looked down the road. About a quarter of a mile away, past several dozen rows of peach trees, was the little cinder-block house the Reyes family lived in. They had helped tend the peach orchards last year and after fall harvest had planned to return to their home in Mexico. However, the patriarch of the family, Ricardo Reyes, had become ill and died. Heartsick and alone with three children to care for, his wife, Marta, asked if they could stay on until spring. Ann had planned to visit the family that morning. She wanted to ensure they had all they needed for a bountiful Christmas. With Sienna's disappearance, she hadn't followed through.

Anjelita, the Reyes's German shepherd, bounded down the lane toward Ann, her paws kicking up little puffs of snow as she ran. Ann's heart thumped in concern when the dog continued to issue sharp barks. Anjelita had never barked at her before. Maybe a welcoming woof, but nothing as urgent as her tone now seemed to imply.

"Anjelita," Ann called out. "It's just me."

When the dog reached her side, Ann stooped down to stroke the animal's head. But Anjelita refused to be petted and began to bark with even more fervor. She broke away from Ann's touch and ran a few yards in the direction of the house. Then she darted back to Ann, only to turn quickly and start toward the house a second time. It appeared the dog was trying to get Ann to follow her.

"Okay, Anjelita," Ann said, "I'm coming." A single light in the kitchen window of the little house shining as her beacon, she hurried down the road in the gathering darkness.

Ann caught up to the dog within a few yards of the house. The front door burst open, and Marta's son, Rogelio, bundled in several layers of clothing, stepped out into the cold. A second bundled figure followed him. Ann strained to make out the features of the person's face. Tendrils of long, dark hair trailed from beneath a colorful woolen stocking cap.

"Aunt Ann?"

The figure bolted towards her. In shock, Ann pulled up short and clasped her hands together. "Sienna?" She opened her arms as her niece fell into her embrace. Anjelita barked and ran circles around them. "Sienna, is it really you? Are you okay?"

"Oh, Aunt Ann. I'm fine. The Reyeses have taken such good care of me. I'll never be able to thank them enough. And Anjelita—" Sienna dropped to her knees to put an arm around the dog's neck. "—how can I ever thank you? You found me and now you've brought Aunt Ann."

Ann knelt down next to Sienna. After ruffling the fur on Anjelita's head, she reached out to touch Sienna's cheek. "I've never been so happy to see anyone," she whispered. "We've got to get you home. Will you be okay here a while longer while I go get the car?"

"I'm okay to walk. I want to come with you," Sienna insisted. "Rojelio went to the farmhouse to get help this morning. He said no one was home. Where is everyone?"

Ann bobbed her head up and down. "Out looking for you."

"Sorry, Marta thought I still needed to rest." She held up her mittened hands. "I just barely convinced her I was well enough to go with Rojelio to find you and Uncle Mark."

After hugging and thanking each member of the Reyes family, Ann and Sienna set off for the farmhouse. From inside Sienna's coat came a soft whimper.

"It's okay, Fedelina," Sienna whispered. "We're going home."

***

TRISH THRUST HER STILL-GLOVED hands into the pockets of her coat. With the sun going down, the cold closed in like a block of ice. Her cell phone was still in her purse. A few minutes ago, she'd pulled it out to check for calls. To her astonishment, there were nearly a dozen from Paul, but she didn't want to return them. She didn't need to feel more hurt than she already did.

She quickened her pace. No cars passed her, and it was nearly dark. As she'd checked the messages, she found that the strength she'd felt when she'd confronted Lynette begin to seep away. She thought about calling for help but realized there wasn't anyone to call. Under the circumstances—with Paul leaving her—she couldn't very well ask him to come get her. Sienna surely wouldn't come. And she couldn't expect Lexie to drop everything and pick her up either. Lexie would be getting everyone ready for the Christmas program. *The Christmas program.* After the way she'd treated everyone at the center, what made Trish think she still even had a right to show up at the tabernacle—even if she could somehow get there on time?

In the distance, the old bridge seemed to beckon. She started toward it but was interrupted by . . . chickens. Chickens clucking "Jingle Bells." A weak smile lifted the corners of her mouth. She pulled the phone from her purse. On the screen flashed an object.

A bright pink heart.

CHAPTER 19

ANOTHER WHIMPER AND THE PUPPY wriggled its head up through the neck of Sienna's coat. Ann chuckled. "Stowaway?"

"Aunt Ann, meet Fedelina."

Ann reached over and scratched the puppy's chin. "Welcome to the family, Fedelina."

Overhead, the evening sky was adorned with brilliant stars. Sienna picked one of them, the biggest and brightest, and made a wish. Despite the encroaching cold and her close call, she felt warm and joyful. She'd been given another chance in more ways than one.

She looked at her aunt and smiled. "I can hardly wait to see my dad . . . and my mom."

Ann jerked her head toward her niece.

"I have so much to tell you," Sienna said, her words and breath turning into a steamy vapor as she spoke. "Aunt Ann, do remember last year when Jamie left so suddenly?"

"Yes. Why?"

"You know in high school I used to go to Uncle Mike's house all the time to see her, mostly when I was mad at my mom. She hated it when I went there. She thought I'd end up drinking like Mike and Jamie." Sienna stopped. With one hand, she held the now-sleeping puppy snugly inside her coat. She put her other hand on her aunt's arm. "Aunt Ann, I know that you know Aunt Jamie wasn't at all like my mom thought she was and that she gave up drinking a long time ago. What you didn't know was that she was obsessed with my mother."

"Obsessed? What do you mean, Sienna?"

"She was convinced my mom needed help."

Ann laughed nervously. "Aren't we all."

"We started talking, and I realized there were lots of things wrong."

"Like what?"

"Like why there are no baby pictures of her but lots of you and Uncle Robert—newborn and toddler pictures. The only pictures I've ever seen of my mom are when she's older. Then there's the fact that when Grandma Kate's mother, Millie, died, her obituary only listed one daughter—Margaret. I was only seven, but I remember my mom cut it out of the paper and kept it in her dresser. Lots of times, when she didn't think I was looking, I saw her holding it and crying. Once I asked her why, and why we never spent any time with Millie, since she was my great-grandmother. Mom would just shake her head, put it away, and tell me it wasn't important. But then I talked to Sam . . . you know how close we've always been."

"What did Sam say, Sienna?"

"Sam said he once overhead you and Uncle Mark talking about how Millie had three daughters. Neither of us understood that, and Sam said when he asked, you didn't answer." Sienna looked over at her aunt. "It's okay. Sam and I both know there are lots of family secrets no one is supposed to talk about."

"Oh, Sienna. I never considered how all of this would affect you kids. How it would affect Sam, my own son. So what did you and Sam decide to do about the 'secrets'?"

"That's where Aunt Jamie came in. She felt like whatever was wrong with Mom was rooted in her childhood and had something to do with Millie. We knew for sure she had two daughters— Grandma Kate and Margaret—and that if Grandma Kate wasn't listed in her obituary, it was possible there really was another daughter out there somewhere. Jamie decided to find out. She went back to Omaha and asked Grandma Kate. She found out a few things. It wasn't much, but it was enough to convince her that Mom was hiding from something. That's why she went to the house a few days before Christmas last year."

"Things are so complicated, Sienna. There's a lot I should tell you, but it's not my place. Your mom—it's really up to her."

"I know. But for some reason she's afraid. She thinks we'll judge her."

"True. She doesn't know how to talk about what's bothering her."

"But I can see that she's trying to make changes," Sienna said. "Did you know that she's taken over almost everything Aunt Jamie was doing at the Providence Center?"

"Don't take this wrong, but are you sure?"

"Didn't you read the article in this week's paper about her? About all she's done to get the kids involved in the community Christmas program?"

"I haven't read it yet. I knew she'd volunteered there, but your mother, involved in the community Christmas program? Usually Lynette Campion's involved with that. I'd think your mom would want to stay as far away as—" Ann stopped short. "You're sure your mom arranged for the kids to be involved?"

"Yes. Her name was right there in the paper: Trish Ingram. Now come on!" Sienna started walking again, pulling Ann along with her. "I went to the Providence Center on Thanksgiving. I wanted to see if there was anything I could do to help the kids and their families. And there she was. I started talking to her and Lexie and found out she's been volunteering there since February. She gradually took on more and more until she was almost running the whole thing. Lexie said she'd been working almost day and night to talk to people to get grants for things the center needs. At first, I wondered why she didn't tell us what she was doing. Then, as I thought about it, I wondered, why didn't we ask? I mean, Dad and I knew she was doing some kind of volunteer work these past several months, but we didn't know where or with who." Sienna's voice dropped. "She was just gone all the time, and we were hurt. We didn't stop to give her the benefit of the doubt and consider that, in her own way, she was really trying to change after Aunt Jamie's death."

Sienna studied her aunt's face in the starlight. There was no sign of joy, like she'd hoped there would be. Instead, her eyes seemed to be fixed on some inner thought, and Ann simply continued walking with her hands deep in her coat pockets.

"Aunt Ann, is something wrong?"

"You know, with nearly the whole county out looking for you, I really thought someone would come along by now and pick us up." Ann looked back over her shoulder toward the highway. "I came home to fix dinner for the kids. Your Uncle Mark headed back out with your dad. Neither of them even stopped to eat."

Ann took her hands out of her pockets and gestured dramatically as she spoke. "I can't believe I didn't even bring my cell phone with me. You know, you still haven't told me what happened. Were you with the Reyes family all this time? I can't believe you were so close! I really should have had you wait there until I got the car . . . are you sure you're okay?"

Sienna slowed her pace and took a hold of her aunt's arm once again. "I'm fine. You didn't answer my question. I can tell by the way you're acting that something's wrong."

Ann kept walking. "Honey, come on. We're almost there."

"Aunt Ann." Sienna stopped, refusing to take another step. The puppy began to squirm in its close quarters, poking its nose up at the neck of Sienna's coat.

Ann turned to face Sienna. "What did you say the puppy's name was?"

"Fedelina. I'm not budging until you tell me what's going on. I thought you'd be happy about what I told you. I don't understand why you're not."

Ann took a deep breath. "Honey, I am happy." She held her hands out, her palms up. "I love your mother more than she'll ever know. I want to think, just as much as you do, that she's capable of returning that love. Not just to strangers but to us, her family. But I don't know that she is. I've spent so many years trying to be a sister and a friend to her, and she . . . she can be so *hard!* It's like getting hit upside the head with a shovel. You love the person who's holding the shovel, but you reach a point where you just can't let yourself be hit anymore." Ann pressed her hands against her chest. "Do you understand what I'm saying?"

"I think she realized a lot after Aunt Jamie talked to her last Christmas." Sienna took the puppy from her coat and put it down on the ground for a moment. "She was trying, Aunt Ann. She was trying to give what Aunt Jamie called the gift. I can see now that she was giving it freely to others, and maybe she just hadn't figured out how to give it to us. Maybe we hadn't given her enough time."

Ann moved closer to Sienna. "I don't want to dampen your enthusiasm about your mom, but . . ." Ann put her hands on Sienna's shoulders. "Today, when your dad went to the house to tell her you were missing, your mother wasn't there. Your dad still can't get in touch with her. He thinks she's disappeared, like he thinks you've disappeared."

"How long has she been gone? Did he try her cell?"

"No one knows for certain how long she's been gone. And, yes, he tried her cell. There was no answer. Sienna, he's worried there's been some sort of foul play. If you ask me, I think your mother is responsible for her own 'disappearance.' I think she just up and left."

"Oh no." Sienna began to shake. She picked up the puppy and stroked its head and ears, cuddling it for comfort. "This is because of me."

"No, Sienna. You certainly can't blame yourself for it."

Tears stung Sienna's eyes. Her voice crackled like newspaper. "Sunday night, when she was away visiting someone, I left an envelope for her under the Christmas tree. She must have opened it. I was only trying to help. We've got to find her!" The puppy back inside her coat, Sienna began to run toward the farmhouse.

"Envelope," Ann puffed at her side, "what envelope?"

Sienna didn't answer.

On the graveled drive that led past the north side of the yard, Sienna saw a handful of cars, trucks, and motorcycles. Several people were moving about between them. In the glow of the yard light on the barn, she recognized one person in particular.

"Daddy!"

She saw her father's head snap to attention as he recognized her voice. Running toward her, he met her on the east side of the barn. "Sienna? Sienna! Where have you been?"

His tears fell freely onto his motorcycle jacket as he pulled her into his arms. Within seconds, they were surrounded by men Sienna recognized as members of Bikers for Families. As they slapped her father on the back, none of them tried to hide the fact they were crying, too.

"Sienna, are you okay? Are you hurt?"

"Careful," Sienna advised as she took Fedelina out of her coat, "don't squeeze us too tight."

Her father smiled through his tears. "And here I was, worried about you being all alone."

Sienna handed the puppy to one of the bikers then took off the gloves Rogelio had loaned her. She grasped her father's hands in hers. "Dad, we've got to find Mom."

Ann put her arm around Sienna's shoulder. "I told her, Paul," Ann whispered.

"It'll be okay," her father said, gathering Sienna into his arms again. "Right now, we've got to get you inside—make sure you're okay."

"Dad, I *am* okay. I want to help find Mom. It's my fault she's gone. I left an envelope at the house." She turned to Ann. "I got a box from Grandma Kate last week. I had written a letter to her on the first of December. I told her that I knew Aunt Jamie had gone to see her last year. I told her I wanted to know more about Mom and Millie and whatever it was that had happened—I told her I had to know the truth. The box she sent—there were some things in it . . . I put them into the envelope. I hoped they'd *help* Mom. But I'm afraid they didn't. I'm afraid they only upset her more."

"Sienna, what was in the envelope?" her father asked.

Sienna explained how Jamie had visited Grandma Kate in Omaha. She kept speaking until it was all out—things she'd hoped her mother would have told her and her father, things she'd learned when Grandma Kate had called her on Sunday. She prayed her father would understand. As she spoke, the look on his face told her he did. She finished by explaining what she'd left in the envelope and why. Beside her, she realized her aunt was quietly weeping.

"Ann?" Paul whispered, his voice gravely and strained. "Is this true? You and Trish . . . are cousins? Why wouldn't she tell me? Why didn't you ever say anything?"

"Forgive me, Paul. It was my parents' decision and then, when Trish found out . . . I tried not to second-guess her, to only hope for the best. The longer we all lived the lie, the harder it was—especially for Trish. I'm so sorry."

Paul blew out a long sigh.

"Paul," Ann said. "I'll see to Sienna. Sienna, you have to let your father go alone. He can get there fastest on his bike. After what you've told us, I think I know where she is. At the bridge."

"Dad." Sienna caught her father's arm as he turned to leave. "I went to the house yesterday to get some decorations for a couple of trees. I'll tell you about that later. Mom left a plate of cookies on the table; I'm sure they were for you." From her pocket she brought out a wadded piece of napkin. Inside were the crumbled pieces of a macadamia-and-white-chocolate chip cookie. "Sorry. I was hungry."

***

IT WAS ALL MAKING SENSE NOW.

Deep in thought, Paul rode through the dark night, speeding on the straightaways and taking corners faster than he should have. He remembered how last year at this time, a couple of days before Christmas, Trish had told him that something special had happened. She promised to tell him about it right after the holidays, when things weren't so hectic and they could sit down and talk uninterrupted.

His uncle and aunt from Colorado had spent Christmas with them and, despite having a house full of company, Trish seemed to enjoy herself. Paul had been intrigued. She seemed softer in her mannerisms, approachable . . . peaceful.

The day after Christmas, however, he'd had to leave on an unexpected overseas business trip that extended into the second week of January. During that time, Mike's wife, Jamie, was hospitalized and passed away. He'd cut his trip short, and in the ensuing days and weeks, his time had revolved around helping his brother make funeral preparations and cope with the loss. He didn't have a spare moment to talk to Trish. Their relationship again became stress filled, and their conversations were often like walking through a minefield, neither of them knowing where it was safe to step. At the time, he felt he couldn't help Mike and simultaneously deal with Trish.

To add to everything, at the funeral, Trish did something so odd, so irrational, he still couldn't comprehend it. He knew she'd sensed his dismay and confusion; he could see it in her eyes and in the way she'd pulled away from his touch.

Turning west off Highway 89 toward I-15, he shifted his body forward on the motorcycle as if the position could help him get to Trish faster.

She never had explained what happened to her before Christmas, but their lack of communication wasn't just her fault. He could have asked her. He could have tried to talk to her about what had happened at the funeral and why she'd acted the way she had, couldn't he? He gunned the bike toward the on-ramp. Driving north on the interstate, he answered his own question: no. Over the years, he'd learned it was not a good idea to bring up things Trish didn't want to talk about. It only made her retreat into her own world, further from his reach.

Besides, there just hadn't been an opportunity. He swallowed hard and admitted to himself that it hadn't been a priority.

Shortly after Jamie's funeral, Trish had started spending enormous amounts of time away from home. Even though a change was evident in her personality—a sort of soft vibrancy that hadn't been there before—he could tell she wasn't keen on broaching any type of deep discussion with him or Sienna.

Now everything was coming into focus. He only prayed he could reach his wife in time. If Ann was right, Trish was in Corinne—at the Bear River Bridge.

***

"HELLO!" TRISH SHOUTED INTO THE phone. "Carrie, is that you?"

"T.D.?" The voice on the other end of the phone crackled. "Where are you?"

"Never mind that. Where are you?"

"I'm at the Providence Center. We're all waiting for you."

"You're—how did you get there? Everyone thought you were

gone—the police thought you'd run away. The school found a note."

"Yeah, pretty stupid, huh? I'm sorry, T.D. My brother said he was going to move out and go to Arizona with some friends. He said he'd called the state and they were on their way to get me. He said I'd have to go back to foster care because he just couldn't hack playing mom anymore. I didn't want to go back. I freaked. I left the note, thinking maybe the cops wouldn't look so hard for me if they thought I was . . . gone. But I didn't know where to go. Sunday night, I broke in and holed up in the basement here. I thought I'd hide until the weekend, then figure out what I was going to do—run, I guess, steal cash out of the safe and hit the road."

"Oh, Carrie. You've been there all the time? I heard that mechanical noise in the background when you left the message last night—it was the old furnace in the basement! I was so scared for you, afraid your leaving was my fault, afraid I'd pushed you too hard."

For a moment, there was silence on the line. "No, T.D., you believed in me. When I was in the basement, all I could think about was how sad you'd be if I left. I remembered what you always told me about Plato, about everyone fighting a battle, and about how even you were fighting one. How one day you'd tell me what it was. I remember how you said that we both had to keep fighting no matter what. Just thinking about it got me through the night. I figured I couldn't just steal the money and run—I knew you'd be disappointed—and I didn't want to quit. I didn't know what I was going to do. Then today, I heard everyone upstairs. I snuck up and listened. They said you'd gotten upset and left last night."

"Yes. I wasn't a very good example, was I? But Carrie, please know this. I didn't stop fighting, and I am proud—so proud—that you didn't stop fighting either."

"T.D., where are you?" Trish heard a break in Carrie's voice and then a sob. "Are you okay? I—we—don't know what we'd do without you. I didn't want to turn myself in to Lexie and the cops. I figured they'd haul me off, but I knew I had to help you. Please come back. Please don't be mad at me."

"Honey, listen. I'm not mad at you at all. I've had some car trouble, that's all. Do me a favor, please? Help Lexie get everyone together, just like we practiced. I'll meet you at the tabernacle. I just have one more thing to do."

CHAPTER 20

FEAR WAS AN EMOTION TRISH knew well; it had been her lifelong companion. Fear of failure had caused her great sorrow and grief. Fear of her past being revealed had persuaded her to lie. Fear of not being understood and accepted had convinced her to mold herself into a cold, hardened creature who vigilantly kept others from getting too close to her. But perhaps because she'd witnessed it firsthand at such a tender age, her fear of death was the most overpowering of all.

Beneath a grayish moon half-sheathed in hazy clouds, fear wasn't simply an emotion. Filling her nostrils and seeping into her lungs, crawling along the inside of her skin with its frigid touch, it was part of her.

At the west end of the bridge, Trish stood alone, her mouth gaping open as she drew jagged gasps of air into her lungs.

It was completely dark now, and the murky expanse of water that was the Bear River flowed restlessly by, obscured by a thin blanket of fog. Trish could not only hear the sound of the water lapping at the riverbank a few feet away, she could sense the river, taste it, smell it.

Like fear, memories of the river had been with her all her life.

Every few minutes a set of headlights flashed on the highway. Their ghostly radiance illuminated the silhouettes of the bridge's steel girders, casting ominous shadows on the ground at her feet. Apprehension seemed to splinter inside her like small shards of glass. Never had she imagined actually being here—again.

Trish cocked her head to one side, straining to hear something more than the impatient river. Her pulse throbbed in her temples, making her light-headed. Each time she exhaled, her breaths formed small white puffs of steam that mingled with the dense fog rising up from the river.

She took a few tenuous steps forward. She couldn't shake the overwhelming feeling that she was about to meet her destiny, whatever it may be.

The wind began to swirl around her. Trish wasn't dressed for the late December evening. Before she zipped up her coat, she took off her gloves so she could draw her sweater together and button it. On impulse, she reached into the right pocket. There was something inside—the Christ child from Sienna's nativity. Somehow, after all she'd been through that day, it was still there.

The wind near the river increased and, for a moment, threatened to throw her off balance. She reached up to push her hair back from blowing into her eyes and, in the process, dropped her gloves. She looked down to where she thought they had fallen. Just inches from her feet was a dark, gaping hole. The gloves had fallen through into the water below.

Steadying herself, she carefully took a few steps in the opposite direction, away from the hole. She could see straight ahead for a short distance. Checking to be sure there were firm pieces of wooden planking beneath her feet, she moved forward. As she did, she started piecing together what likely happened on that night, forty years ago—the third anniversary of when her father, Thomas Clark, had died in Vietnam. Her mother had left her with Bessie. Then, when Bessie put things together and realized Cecile's intentions, she went after her on foot, carrying Trish . . .

Trish forced herself to search her memories, back to her adolescence when she and Lynette were teenagers. They'd met on the first day of junior high in P.E. and, from the start, Trish sensed Lynette knew something she didn't. When the class had embarked on a swimming session, Trish balked at getting into the pool. Lynette, then a total stranger to her, remarked that she wasn't surprised.

"If I were you," she'd told Trish, "I'd be scared of the water, too. You, more than anyone, have a good reason to be afraid."

How did Lynette know she *was* afraid of the water? At the time, Trish didn't even know why. Then there were the remarks

Lynette made about orphans and children who had no clue as to who their real parents were. But she dropped the real bombshell at a slumber party right before Halloween.

To set the mood, Lynette turned out the light in her room and invited the other girls to share scary stories. When they were all fidgeting with fright, Lynette announced she had the best story of all. It was the true account of a woman who'd jumped to her death from the Bear River Bridge.

Trish shuddered. Even though decades had elapsed, the details of Lynette's malicious narrative pierced her mind like a knife. In a macabre tone, Lynette had told how the suicidal woman, estranged from her family, had returned one last time to her childhood home to seek forgiveness from her mother for all her wrongdoings. When her mother refused to accept her apologies, she felt she had no other option but to throw herself from the bridge.

Could it be true? Had her mother asked her grandmother for forgiveness one last time? Trish reached up to touch the wetness on her cheek.

All her life she'd believed her mother had come here to commit suicide with no regard for what might happen after she jumped. She'd believed her mother didn't care what happened to her in the aftermath or whether she fell into the river herself. But this afternoon, she'd learned that her mother had left her in a safe place—with Bessie—her paternal grandmother. Her mother wasn't as calloused as Trish had thought her to be, as calloused as Lynette had said.

It was in the weeks following the slumber party, following additional malicious remarks—sugarcoated like bitter medicine Lynette wanted her to swallow—that Trish had put two and two together. One night, while Kate and John were away, Trish snuck into Kate's cedar chest and found a photo album. Inside were two photos that showed Trish as a baby in the arms of a woman who was clearly *not* Kate—the same photos she'd found this morning in the envelope, along with a birth certificate that said someone named Cecile Ann Anderson was her mother. The space intended for a father's name had been left blank.

The shock had been nearly unbearable. The people whom she believed to be her parents were her aunt and uncle. They had lied—her life was a lie. Kate had tried hard to comfort her, but Trish was angry, bitterly angry. She wouldn't speak to Kate or John for months. She wouldn't even speak to Ann and Robert. They'd lied to her. She'd hated them.

Even later, when Kate had tried to explain, Trish hadn't wanted to hear it. All she knew for certain was that her mother was Kate's younger sister. She hadn't wanted to know anything more, though bits and pieces filtered in through conversations over the years. She'd been unrelentingly rude to Kate and John—hateful, even. She realized now how very selfish that was.

As suddenly as it swelled, the wind stopped, and the sound of the river filled Trish's ears. She forced herself to take several steps forward.

After Lynette had so brutally exposed her past, Kate had tried to explain about her mother and the circumstances surrounding her death. But Trish had been so steeped in contempt that she'd made up her mind to hate her mother as much as she hated the McClures.

And why?

She stopped walking, the mist closing in for a moment. Jamie had been right after all. Providence. She had been watched over. Kate and John had been as good to her as any parents could be. Ann and Robert loved her. Paul and Sienna tried their best to love her as well. Even Bessie had said she had loved her from a distance—a guardian angel Trish didn't even know she had. And there had been more. The footprints at Mike's. The phone showing up in the attic. Randall asking for her. She couldn't deny that her life had indeed been blessed.

The mist continued to swirl and roll, parting again to reveal the surface of the bridge. Though small splotches remained here and there, the warmth of the day had melted away the bulk of the snow. In Trish's moonlit view, she could see that several more pieces of the wooden planking were missing. Carefully sidestepping the missing planks, Trish tried not to look down through gaping holes like the one where her gloves had fallen through. Once the only travel route into Corinne, the bridge, due to its dangerous state of decay, was now permanently closed to vehicles. A few feet back, there had been a sign stating that pedestrian traffic was strictly prohibited as well.

Trish made her way over to the left railing of the bridge. The flat metal was deathly cold to her touch. The mist undulated beneath the planking, cloaking the water and making it appear as though it wasn't there, as though there was nothing but dead space. Had it been this way the night her mother died? Had the fog, concealing the river, made it easier for her to jump?

Every few seconds, fingers of mist curled up over the wooden planking. Navigating a safe path was difficult. Trish exhaled and moved forward. She didn't know why, but she felt certain Cecile had gone to the center of the bridge and drowned near the middle of the river. She had to get to that spot. "Mama, I'm so sorry," Trish whispered.

Like an eraser wiping chalk from a chalkboard with one efficient sweep, Trish found her fear gone and replaced by determination. Everything had come full circle. She had to see this through.

The wind picked up again. A heavy fog closed in on the bridge. Trish waited. It didn't dissipate. She crouched down and brushed her fingers over the wood. The planking in front of her seemed intact. She stood up and took a few more steps. Several feet ahead and to her right, the fog parted. She chose a course that led to that area. Reaching the right side of the bridge, she then attempted to take hold of the railing. Her fingers, stiffened from the cold, would not cooperate.

On each side of her, an eerie glow suddenly formed. It seemed to come from somewhere behind her. Trish stopped and pivoted on her heel. It was a headlight—a single headlight. There were four houses on the city block preceding the bridge, two on each side of the street. They'd been dark and seemingly unoccupied when she'd passed them. The light was probably someone coming home.

Trish turned back toward the center of the bridge and prepared to take another step forward.

"Trish?"

A voice broke through the mist. Trish strained to see through yet another rippling blanket of fog, but it was too thick. She heard footsteps on the bridge.

"Trish? Are you there? Answer me—*please!*"

Trish gasped. The voice she heard was Paul's.

"Paul. I'm here!"

"Trish. Thank heaven. Please stay where you are. Talk to me."

"Paul, be careful! Lots of planks are missing. Let the fog clear." Trish could hear his footsteps. He seemed to be continuing on despite her caution. "Wait! Please! No!" Trish drew in a sharp breath. The words she'd just said—they were the same three words she'd said when Jamie had left the house last Christmas. The same words she'd said to—*Mama!*

Trish remembered now, dreamlike from across the years. She remembered Bessie holding her as they both saw Cecile making her way to the center of the bridge. Reaching out with her little arms to where her mother had disappeared, Trish remembered she'd yelled, "Mama! Wait! Please! No!" But she hadn't been alone. Her mother hadn't callously left her, not caring what became of her. Cecile had no idea Bessie would follow, no idea Trish would be an unwitting observer. Just as with Margaret's death, the things that happened were the result of unfortunate circumstances.

"Oh, Mama!" Trish sobbed. Yielding fully to what Randall—her uncle—had asked of her, giving voice to what she'd intended to do at the cemetery, she cried, "Mama, I love you. I *forgive* you!"

A single, splintering crack shattered the air.

"Paul? Paul!" Trish heard herself scream. Clambering across the planks as her frozen fingers tried to grip the railing, she moved toward the sound. "Paul. Oh, Father in Heaven—no. Not Paul!"

Tears cascaded down her cheeks. Terror pulsed through her veins. But then the moon broke through the clouds. The mist parted briefly, and she almost collapsed with relief. Just a few yards ahead she could see her husband. He walked toward her and gathered her into his arms. She leaned into his warmth.

"The wood—I heard the crack . . . I thought you'd fallen into the river." She sobbed.

"I just stepped in the wrong place. But there was a woman . . . she showed me the way. It's okay now. Everything's going to be fine."

"A woman? Where?"

"I don't know where she went, but I'll never forget her. She was wearing a long white coat."

***

HER HAIR MATTED AND WET, her makeup smeared, Trish stood at the podium of the tabernacle. Paul's jacket hung loosely on her shoulders, the black leather dotted with melting snowflakes, the result of her first-ever motorcycle ride. It was exactly seven thirty.

Whispers spread through the audience like wildfire. Some people laughed. Some pointed. Many murmured and shook their heads. From one of the balcony seats came a sharp bark from Sienna's puppy. Trish smiled and tapped the microphone.

"Mr. Cook has graciously allowed me a few minutes of your time. I, like the rest of you, have been deeply touched by the song we've just heard, 'Goodwill Toward Men.' These kids have worked hard. They set a goal and reached it. They believed in themselves; they had faith. I want to thank them for their examples." She took a deep breath. "Mr. Cook asked me to announce that there's been a change in the program. Our featured guest soloist, Lynette Campion, has not yet arrived. I hope she will join us shortly."

The murmurs increased, but Trish proceeded, undaunted.

"Instead, we will be blessed with the opportunity to hear from a special men's choir. But first, I have something else to say." She could see the crowd shift uncomfortably in their seats, but she knew she might never have the opportunity again. She looked down at the first row into Paul's face. He smiled warmly and gave her the thumbs-up.

"Even though I live in Cache Valley, many of you here know me, and have known me, over the years, as a proud, stubborn woman, a woman of misguided prejudice and harshness." That statement garnered a few snickers. Trish cleared her throat. "But none of you has ever known what is in my heart.

"I've lived my life in fear of many things. I was convinced I couldn't survive without . . . material things. But I deceived myself. I'm here tonight to tell you, true happiness does not come from the things of this world or from the fleeting approval of others." Trish gripped the podium. "It comes from knowing who you are and embracing that knowledge, from knowing that what you're doing is right regardless of what others might say, from doing the Lord's will.

"Sometimes bad things happen. Sometimes we get hurt. But we must not give in to despair and succumb to being individuals our Father in Heaven would not be proud of. To quote Luke, *'Be ye therefore merciful, as your Father also is merciful. Judge not, and ye shall not be judged: condemn not, and ye shall not be condemned: forgive, and ye shall be forgiven.'*"

Trish paused for moment, her tears falling onto the podium. "Last year, a very wise woman—my sister-in-law, Jamie Ingram, who started the Providence Center—told me something that changed my life. She came to my door just before Christmas and gave me the most important gift I have ever received. It was the gift of love. Not only is this gift available from our friends and family, if we will but recognize and accept it, but the Lord offers it to all of us as well. Accepting it and learning to love ourselves as He does is the most important thing we can do.

"On this, the third night before the eve of Christmas, when we will celebrate His birth, let us all strive to remember that we can give what He gave." Trish took a deep breath and said with conviction, "Give *the* gift."

The words echoed through the tabernacle. As Trish finished speaking, a line of men in black leather jackets, leather leggings, and boots filed in to surround her at the podium. She nodded to the pianist. Any curious stares or expressions of shock over the men's appearances were quickly replaced as their voices flowed softly through the hall.

"Silent night! Holy night! All is calm, all is bright . . . "

Near the end of the song, the sweet sound of a woman's voice mingled with those of the bikers—Lynette's. She finished with "Panis Angelicus."

> *Per tuas semitas*
> *duc nos quo tendimus,*
> *Ad lucem quam inhabitas.*
>
> *By your ways,*
> *lead us who seek*
> *the light in which you dwell.*

CHAPTER 21

TRISH SAT IN FRONT OF a blazing fire in the family room. Tomorrow, Lexie and all the kids from the Providence Center would come for Christmas dinner. Tonight was Christmas Eve. She looked around at everyone who had come to spend the evening with her. Ann pounded out "Jingle Bells" on the piano while her daughter Sarah and Marta's daughters Belicia and Calida laughed and joined Sienna in trying to sing the song in both English and Spanish. Tears formed in Trish's eyes. Oh, how grateful she was for her sister and daughter and the woman who had helped saved Sienna's life.

A group of bikers was in the kitchen, seated at the breakfast bar. Not having families of their own, they enjoyed being fussed over by Bessie. And, at the kitchen table, Ann's husband, Mark, and their two sons, Sean and Sam, played a raucous game of Go Fish with Rogelio.

Paul and Mike sat huddled on one of the overstuffed sofas in the family room, talking about old times and planning fishing trips for the future. Paul looked over at Trish and smiled.

She touched the heart-shaped diamond pendant he had placed around her neck earlier that day. It had been under the tree in a blue velvet box. Trish tipped her head back, listening to the sounds of her family and friends laughing, loving, and enjoying life. With the smells of hot chocolate and Bessie's molasses cookies almost ready to pull from the oven, it was just like heaven.

Happy. Yes, Jamie, now I'm happy. Thank you.

When Trish motioned Sienna to follow her, Sienna handed her puppy over to the younger girls and left the piano as they started a new song.

"I'll be back in a minute," Trish told Paul. She took Sienna by the hand and walked into the entryway. Reaching into the pocket of her sweater, she pulled out the tiny Christ child. "I thought you should be the one to put Him back in the manger."

"Thanks, Mom." Sienna took the figurine from Trish's hands and lovingly laid it in the matchbox manger. "Do you think Stephanie will be able to be with us next year?"

"Yes, I'm praying she will be," Trish said. Glancing back down the hallway to the kitchen and family room, she added, "I'm praying there'll be a lot more here next Christmas Eve."

"Like Uncle Randall?" Sienna asked.

"Yes." Trish smiled. "Like Uncle Randall. It's truly a miracle. I spoke with the doctor at the hospital about an hour ago. He said Randall's condition is steadily improving. By tomorrow morning, they think he'll be able to come off the oxygen. I'm holding out hope they'll let me take him Christmas dinner. Bessie and I are going to run back to the hospital to check on him in a few minutes . . . I don't want him to be alone."

"Mind if I go with you?" Sienna put her arm around her mother.

"I was hoping you would. But before we go there's something I need to show you. Grab a trash bag from the kitchen, if you will, please, and come upstairs."

Sienna gave her a quizzical look before grabbing the bag and following Trish to the hallway that overlooked the family room. There, they paused briefly to wave at those gathered below before continuing up the stairs to the attic. Trish maneuvered through the boxes then sat down on the vanity bench.

"What's all this?" Sienna scrunched up her face as she studied the photos on the dresser mirror.

"For a very long time, these women were my ideals of strength and success."

Sienna grimaced. "Lynette Campion?"

Trish laughed. "She's trying, Sienna. Here, hand me the bag." Keeping a couple of the pieces of tape, Trish yanked all the photos down and, without hesitation, tossed them into the trash bag.

Picking up the letter, she started reading out loud from where she'd left off.

"*. . . By now, Trisha, you must be a beautiful young woman. Full of the light and life that has always been in your eyes. When you were* *born, I knew God must have loved me at least a little to send down His most beautiful and choice angel to my arms. Never forget that I will always love you."*

Trish pulled the two photos of her and her mother from the envelope and taped them on the mirror. Touching her fingers to her lips and then to the photos, she whispered, "I love you too, Mama."

She looked at Sienna. "I want to put up new photos—of you, Bessie, Grandma Kate, and Ann. *You* are the women I want to be like. You are my ideals of strength and success."

Sitting down next to Trish on the bench, Sienna hugged her mother. Together they looked into the mirror at their reflections and smiled.

EPILOGUE

March 4, 2011

STEPHANIE INGRAM MADE FACES, EVEN at complete strangers, leaving them to wonder why a little girl would do such a thing. She threw things and kicked things, like the pail that held the chicken feed. She hated feeding the chickens. She hated chickens, period. All they did was squawk and fuss and become upset when she entered their coop.

On Friday, with California's early spring sun beating down on her head, Stephanie walked out and dumped the chicken mash onto the floor of the coop. Though Grandpa had told her time and again to put it in the metal feed containers he'd set out for his prize laying hens, she didn't care where the mash landed—dumb chickens, anyway. Then she dumped fresh water from a bucket *in the general direction* of the round water dispensers the chickens drank from. Most of the water ended up making a muddy mess on the floor of the coop.

Who cared?

In the back of her head, she could hear her grandfather's voice. *"Stephanie, I need you to unscrew the tops of the containers, turn them, and fill them up. Then screw the bottoms back on and flip them over. That way, the chickens will have water for the whole day."*

Stephanie heard the words, but she ignored them. She hated listening too. No one ever said anything new. All they ever told her was how they didn't like what she'd done or that she'd messed up or forgotten something—again.

Though it was barely eight o'clock, the morning was already getting hot. Stephanie hated the coop even more on hot days—the heat made the smell of the chickens unbearable. She pinched her nose for a moment, then hurried and grabbed the hens' eggs. She placed them into the brown wicker basket Grandma had given her to collect them in.

Step, scuff. She slowly moved her feet across the dry, dusty soil of the farmyard back toward the little white frame house. When she came to live with her grandparents last year and first started to collect the eggs, a couple of times she'd stumbled and the eggs had crashed to the ground. She would never forget how it made her feel. To Stephanie, the broken eggs confirmed what she knew everyone else thought of her—she was stupid.

Stephanie stopped walking. Her mouth pursed, her "mean" face on, the one meant to tell the world, "I don't care!"—even if she really did.

People didn't come right out and say they thought she was stupid, but she could see it in their eyes. Like the eyes of her teachers when her math problems didn't add up right or when her penmanship looked more like the scratches the chickens made in the dirt than how a kid was supposed to write on a piece of paper. She could also hear it in the laughter of the kids in her class when she read out loud and made mistakes in pronunciation.

And she could hear it in the voice of her mother.

Even though she hadn't seen her mother in well over two years, she could still hear her voice sarcastically reminding her, time and again, to pick up after herself, wipe her mouth, and wash her hands. *"Oh, Stephanie,"* her mother had often said in an irritated tone, *"stand up straight. What will people think of you? Put a smile on your face or no one will like you. Someone like you needs all the friends she can get!"*

Step, scuff. Stephanie started walking again and made her mean face even more severe. Making her mean face was part of being a bad person. While no one ever came right out and told her, "Stephanie, you're a bad person!" she knew it like she knew she was stupid and like she knew that her clothes would never be quite right, that her hair would always be a mess, and that her face wasn't the kind, pretty face people liked to see.

She knew all these things because her mother had abandoned her, and her stepmother, Jamie, had died—allowing God take her to heaven. After that, her dad said he couldn't take care of her anymore, so he'd sent her to live with her grandparents. They only let her stay with them because they had to. Her mother, she'd heard them say late one night, was their only daughter; Stephanie, their only granddaughter—they had no choice.

The eggs rattled in the basket. Stephanie slowed her step. She could probably get by with dumping the mash and water haphazardly—Grandpa wouldn't find out until later. But after the last time of tripping with the eggs and having them splatter all over the ground and her shoes, she set her mind she would never drop them again.

Sometimes, even when she wasn't carrying eggs, she practiced her careful don't-break-the-eggs walk. Although she knew she was bad, knew she was stupid, it didn't mean she needed to show it any more than she did—if she could help it.

She stepped and scuffed. Stepped and scuffed. Little piles of dry, brown earth rose up over the toes of her shoes. Her shoes and socks might be covered with dirt, but at least she wasn't going to drop the eggs.

Nearing the house, she heard a noise behind the lilac bushes at the edge of the grass on her right. She stopped. The noise was high and shrill like a whistle, like none she'd ever heard.

Stephanie put the basket down and walked softly toward the bushes. She knelt down and peered under the green leaves. Two baby birds were on the ground, their nest in pieces, their mother nowhere to be seen.

Her fingers tensed. She'd always wanted to hold a baby bird. She wanted to lunge forward and grab them before they could run. But something stopped her—things usually broke when she held them.

Deciding to wait and watch, she sat on the grass and looked at the babies under the foliage. The gray and white speckled birds seemed to have a lot of feathers, but they also had patches of cottony down that ruffled in the summer breeze. Wobbling on stubby legs, their wings flapped awkwardly at their sides. Their wide fluorescent yellow beaks gaped open and shut as they issued mournful chirps.

Stephanie watched so long she knew it must be well past time for Grandma to start cooking breakfast. Grandma would think she'd dropped the eggs again and that she was trying to hide the shells and come up with another story about how the chickens hadn't lain. She made her mean face. Grandma would just have to think that. It did, however, make her sad to think of Grandma with an empty pan and no eggs.

Grandma was getting old. It was hard for her to walk even short distances with her cane. It was much too far for her to walk to the coop to check on Stephanie. In a few minutes Grandpa would be ready for breakfast. He'd come looking for Stephanie if she didn't show up.

The baby birds began to call more urgently. Where was their mother? Stephanie's brow wrinkled in anger. Typical. Mothers were never around when you needed them.

Her own stomach growling, she realized the babies must be hungry. She stood and ran back to the coop, where she got the empty chicken mash pail and headed for the garden. Once there, she found an old shovel and turned over a few shovelfuls of dirt, like she'd seen Grandpa do when he worked in the garden.

On the moist underside of the soil were three fat earthworms. Stephanie plucked them out, put them into the pail, and returned to the birds. She'd heard if people touched baby animals, their mothers would never come back, so she took great care to dangle a worm just within reach of their beaks without letting her fingers touch their feathers.

Smelling the worms, the birds pecked at them, but their efforts were awkward. They couldn't obtain even the tiniest of bites.

"Starlings."

Stephanie hadn't heard Grandpa walk up behind her.

"Their mother's gone. They need help. They're starving." Stephanie stood up and gestured frantically.

"Starlings," Grandpa repeated. "Best if they do starve. Best get those eggs into your grandmother," he added, pointing at the basket.

"But . . ." Stephanie made her mean face at Grandpa's back as he turned and went to the house. She kicked the chicken mash pail across the grass. Just then, a silver car pulled into the graveled drive between the barn and the east side of the house. Who was it? Stephanie craned her neck. The car stopped and two women got out.

For a moment, they stood and spoke to Grandpa. Then they began to walk toward her. Stephanie slumped down onto the grass, her arms folded across her stomach. People from the school had come out to the farm last year to tell Grandpa and Grandma how bad she'd been.

By the time they reached her side, she recognized the women as her Uncle Paul's wife and daughter. A few weeks ago, Stephanie had received a letter from her dad telling her they were coming to see her. But he hadn't said when and he hadn't said why. She dropped her chin to her chest and refused to look at them, though she'd always liked it when Sienna used to come visit her and Jamie.

"Stephanie, do you remember me? I'm your Aunt Trish, and this is your cousin Sienna."

Stephanie made her very worst face and said, "So?"

"We've come to talk to you."

"Don't wanna talk. I ain't done nothin' bad, so you can go away."

There was silence, and Stephanie thought they might be going. She lifted her head slightly and saw they were still there.

"Did your dad tell you we were going to come?"

"Maybe."

Silence again. After a few moments, the baby birds started to chirp. Trish and Sienna sat down next to her on the grass.

"Sounds like you've got a couple of friends back there," Sienna said, putting a hand on Stephanie's shoulder.

"I don't have friends." Anger filled Stephanie. She didn't like people being too close, didn't like them touching her. She shrugged Sienna's hand away.

"Can we take a look?" asked Trish.

"Do what you want," Stephanie muttered. "They're just dumb old starlings anyway. Better off if they starve."

Trish and Sienna moved the few feet toward the bushes on their hands and knees. *Stupid.* Why would grown-ups even bother with a couple of birds?

"Looks like somebody cared enough to try and feed them," Sienna said. "There are some worms here."

Stephanie turned her head to the side and looked at the ground. "Sure as heck their mother's not gonna feed them. Mothers are never around."

"I had a baby bird once," Trish said. "I was about your age. It was a baby robin. It fell out of a nest in my Grandpa and Grandma McClure's yard."

"What'd you do?" Stephanie moved her body clockwise on the grass to face Trish and Sienna. "Did you keep it?"

"Well, I got some worms for it, just like these. I fed it a few. Then my grandpa got a piece of sheep's wool and picked it up in that and put it back into the nest." Trish smiled at her. "It was fun to feed it."

"These ones are too stupid to eat the worms, and their nest's all busted up. Their mother's never going to come back. But I didn't touch them," Stephanie said quickly. "I wanted her to come back if she would—but she won't. Mothers never come back."

"Maybe we should try feeding them again. You want to give it a shot?" asked Trish. "They look big enough; I think they could eat the whole worm."

"Sure . . . I guess," Stephanie whispered.

"Okay," instructed her aunt. "Grab the end of the worm, and when they open their beaks, dangle it inside and a little down their throats."

Stephanie picked up a worm and held it until one of the babies opened its beak. She let the worm hang inside its mouth, and within a few seconds the bird gobbled it down. "Hey, it worked!" she cried.

"Great job, Stephanie," said Trish. "Let's try another one."

After the birds finished the worms, Stephanie took her aunt and cousin to the garden. Together, they found three more and put them into the pail.

"Ooooh," laughed Sienna, "slimy worms!" She made a face, but it wasn't a mean face; it was a funny, happy face.

Stephanie let herself smile at her cousin. Sienna was nice. So was Aunt Trish. They made her feel . . . good. Without thinking, she asked, "Do you want to see me carry eggs?" The moment the words left her mouth, she was sorry. How stupid could she be? *Plenty.* Who'd want to see her carry eggs?

"Yes," said Trish. "I bet it takes a special person to do that."

Stephanie was astounded. Was Aunt Trish making fun of her, or was she serious? The look on her face seemed sincere.

Walking to where she'd left the eggs, she gingerly picked up the basket. *Step, scuff.* She was so careful the eggs barely moved. *Step, scuff.* Her aunt and cousin followed her to the house. She opened the screen door and walked into the kitchen. Grandma, who was sitting at the table with Grandpa, nodded her approval; the eggs had arrived unscathed.

Stephanie hardly dared to turn around to see the looks on Aunt Trish's and Sienna's faces. When she did, her heart did a flip-flop. Their faces were happy and smiling.

"Come here, special girl," Trish held out her arms. "That was wonderful!"

For a moment, Stephanie was torn. She wanted, more than she could admit to herself, to run into her aunt's embrace. But, certainly, if not right now, then in the next few minutes, she'd mess up. She'd do or say something to show Aunt Trish how bad and stupid she really was. Then, like all the other people—like her mother—Aunt Trish would hate her.

Stephanie pushed past her and dashed to screen door, hitting it so hard with the heels of her hands that the screen ripped. She rushed outside and to the bushes. She threw herself down next to the baby birds. Startled by her abrupt movements, they tried frantically to wobble away.

"That's right. Go. Just go away!" she screamed. She picked up the chicken mash pail to throw at them.

"You don't really want to do that, do you?"

Trish was by her side.

"I can see you love those birds, Stephanie. You made sure not to touch them because you wanted their mother to come back. You went and found worms to feed them so they wouldn't be hungry."

Stephanie dropped the pail. Trish gathered her into her arms. She didn't resist.

"Stephanie, I don't know why your mother left. Maybe she doesn't even know herself. Sometimes people do things . . ."

Wrenching herself away from her aunt, Stephanie cried, "She did it because I'm bad; because she hates me! Jamie hated me too. That's why she went to live with God."

"When God calls someone home, they have to go, Stephanie. Jamie didn't want to leave you, but God needed her in heaven."

"That's not true. She just didn't want me. Nobody wants me . . . not even my dad!" Trish reached for her. Stephanie shoved her away.

"Your dad does want you. He's just trying to sort out his life right now."

"No! If he wanted me, he wouldn't have left me," Stephanie yelled. "Starlings are supposed to starve and die—Grandpa said so—that's why they're there. Left alone to starve and die. Maybe I am too!" She kicked the pail at her aunt and turned away. Before she knew it, she was running into the chicken coop. She slammed the door shut and pressed herself into a corner.

It was only a matter of seconds before Trish entered the coop as well. She stood in the middle of the floor.

"I can't explain why your grandpa said what he did about the starlings. Different people just have different ideas, Stephanie. It doesn't mean they're right. I can't explain why your mom left and why your dad is having a hard time. I can't even explain why God needed Jamie in heaven." Trish threw her arms toward the ceiling of the coop. "But I know one thing for sure." She brought her hands back down and held them to her chest, over her heart. "*I want you.*"

Her aunt's declaration took Stephanie by surprise. She pressed her forehead against the wood in the corner until it hurt.

"I know you don't remember, but when you were a baby, I was one of the first people who got to hold you. I rocked you in my arms and sang to you, and I made you a promise—a promise that if you ever needed anything I'd be here for you."

Trish moved next to Stephanie and kept talking. "I've always wanted you. I couldn't take you right after Jamie died. I had some things to sort out myself. But I'm here now, and I'm ready to keep my promise." After a moment she said, "Stephanie, I love you, and I want you to come and stay with me and Uncle Paul and Sienna. Sienna and I have fixed the room right next to hers for you."

Stephanie kept her forehead pressed into the corner. She took a couple of deep breaths then pinched her nose shut. With the heat inside the coop, everything smelled horrible.

"You too, huh?" Trish chuckled. "When I tell you this, maybe you can understand how much I love you: I hate chickens, Stephanie. They're my least favorite bird. When I was a little girl and gathered eggs, they chased me and tried to peck at me. It scared me half to death. If I didn't want you, I wouldn't be standing here in this smelly chicken coop, ankle deep in chicken poop with this one pecking at my leg!"

Stephanie moved from the corner and saw a big brown chicken pecking at her aunt's pant leg. She felt a giggle well up in her throat. "Shoo," she urged. Both she and Trish laughed out loud. She took her aunt's hand and led her outside into the fresh air.

"Look," she cried. Across the yard, a bird with shiny black feathers squawked at the baby birds. Their wings flapped with vigor. They stumbled forward, following the larger bird into another section of the lilac bushes.

"Oh, Stephanie. Yes. Their mother did come back for them."

"It might be their mother." Stephanie squeezed Trish's hand tightly and made a happy face. "But I think it's their aunt."

ABOUT THE AUTHOR

Lori Nawyn's short stories, essays, and articles have appeared in numerous publications, including the *Deseret News, Segullah,* and "The SCBWI Bulletin." *My Gift to You* is her first novel. She lives in northern Utah, where she is currently at work on her next book. To learn more about Lori, visit her website at www.lorinawyn.com.